THE
COMMUNITY

THE
COMMUNITY

Jean Spenst

iUniverse, Inc.
Bloomington

The Community

iUniverse books may be ordered through booksellers or by contacting:

iUniverse
1663 Liberty Drive
Bloomington, IN 47403
www.iuniverse.com
1-800-Authors (1-800-288-4677)

ISBN: 978-1-4620-2304-2 (sc)
ISBN: 978-1-4620-2303-5 (hc)
ISBN: 978-1-4620-2305-9 (ebk)

Printed in the United States of America

iUniverse rev. date: 10/06/2011

Acknowledgement

I finally did it. One of my goals was to write a book and get it published. It finally happened. The journey has been fun and I learned a lot.

I want to thank my family and friends that urged me along the way to complete my first book. IUniverse was a great help and also published my story.

A special thanks to Joan Hall Hovey, my instructor, from Winghill Writing School who always gave me wonderful feedback and encouraged me every time I sent in a lesson. Without her assistance I know I wouldn't have been able to complete my story.

I hope you enjoy my story.
HAPPY READING!

Jean Spenst

Chapter One

November

The automobile smashed and bounced along the uneven earth. It was a great feeling to watch as the asshole and his car dove fifty feet to the rugged, uneven ground before hitting the bottom of the coulee. No one would miss him immediately. This opportunity couldn't have worked out any better. While the lookout point was a great addition to this community, Drake didn't expect any sightseers would come this way for a while, as the weather was getting colder and the tourist season was far off. He hoped for a huge snowfall to cover the remodeled '69 Mustang that the slimeball had called his pride and joy. If, by chance, the fall hadn't killed him, the weather and wild animals would do the trick. Drake envisioned the coyotes and maggots feeding on the idiot's remains.

The asshole, he thought, *was a liar. He told everyone he had no money, but he was richer than anyone in this area. Another problem resolved and 'nough of the drama for now.* Drake craved some weed and a good swig of Crown Royal on the rocks to calm his nerves.

Drake breathed in and slowly exhaled as he tried to relieve the pent-up tension in his body. After one last look in the direction of the coulee that now contained a not-so-permanent fixture lying fifty feet below, he turned away from the embankment and walked to his Harley that was parked a few paces away. He lifted a long, lanky leg over the seat and started up the beast, revving the engine to hear the roar of life and feel the vibration of the machine. He was ready to return to Drumheller and relax.

1

He decided to cool it, as a nosy neighbor lived not too far away. Then he remembered she was in town for the day helping out at the old folks' home. She had a nice ass and a set of tits, but it was too bad the rest of her was a mess; otherwise, he wouldn't mind having a piece of it. Knowing she wouldn't appreciate such a fine stud in her presence, he shook those thoughts out of his head and convinced himself that she wouldn't be able to handle him, yeah.

Now that the asshole was out of the way, he would get paid for a job well done. It was time to get his reward. In a few days, he would head back to Calgary.

Chapter Two

As Drake revved the Harley's engine once again, a shiver trailed down his spine. He sensed someone behind him. Slowly he turned his head, fully expecting to see someone, but no one was behind him. He shook his head and laughed nervously. *Man, this is nuts. That was a long way down from the lookout point, and there was no way anyone could have survived such an accident.*

He reached for his sunglasses to protect his eyes from the wind that would attack him on the ride to where he was staying. He put on the glasses, lifted his legs off the ground, and let the bike soar to life.

He approached the main graveled road from the exit of the lookout point and checked for traffic both ways. He turned left and headed to his friend's house where he was going to party that night. In twenty minutes, he would be there.

Man, it feels great being on this bike, he thought as he enjoyed the freedom of the beast. He was fortunate to have a friend who knew how to get great deals on this mode of transportation. Winters sucked, but the summer was just fine with the freedom to ride his bike through towns and villages.

Drake eased down the hill to head toward his destination. He wouldn't be alone much longer, as the big guy would come in from the north. Well, at least he would get paid, although he preferred being by himself without the boss hanging around. Drake didn't like that man, but the money was just fine. He hoped the boss wouldn't be staying long.

Drake drove into the farmyard and up the short, graveled, and bumpy driveway. He pulled up in front of the garage, got off the bike, and turned off the engine. He pushed down the kickstand, lifted his leg over the seat, and walked toward the front door of the house. No need to lock the doors in this neighborhood, which never had any crime—until today. Not really a crime, it was more like getting rid of the garbage. Oops, it was disposed of in the wrong place. Time would take care of the remains.

The house had three big bedrooms, a bathroom, an oversized combination kitchen-dining room, and a large, square living room. The kitchen cabinets were almond-stained oak. The flooring was dark brown linoleum that extended from the kitchen to all of the rooms in the house.

The closest neighbors were approximately two miles away on either side of the house. Drake loved the quiet. Everyone in this neighborhood was friendly, but most kept to themselves just the way he liked it—except for the nosy woman who lived about five miles away. He just ignored her.

Opening the front door, he took the steps two at a time and entered the kitchen. Drake shed his leather jacket and removed his sunglasses. He draped his jacket over the kitchen chair so he could easily grab it on the way out. He sat on that chair and admired his Harley Davidson boots that had been acquired not so long ago. He had friends in low places.

Man, after a job well done, I need to celebrate. Instead of the whiskey, a cold one sounded about right. Getting out of the chair, he made his way to the fridge and reached for his prize of leftover pizza and a cold one. He grabbed a paper towel on the way to the living room so he could watch TV while he relaxed. Without the satellite, he would have had a choice of only three channels that were fuzzy most of the time—man, that would be a drag.

He set his paper towel, the pizza, and his beer on the end table next to the recliner. Grabbing the remote, he turned on the TV and channel surfed until he came to the directory to select a sports channel to watch while he ate.

Yawning after wolfing down his snack and drink, he placed the bottle on the coffee table and stretched out in the recliner. The game was boring, but he wasn't interested in watching anything else. As his eyes began to close, he thought, *This is the life, no one to hassle me and I can enjoy my free time. Man, I've had a hard day.*

Chapter Three

Drake fell asleep as he watched the baseball game. In his dream he rode the beast on the straight and narrow dirt road. The clouds were dark with the hint of rain yet to come. The lightning made quite a show as it advanced toward him. On his Harley the road felt like it pulled him along on his ride. He didn't know where he was.

Another strike of aqua lightning steadily advanced. As he continued to ride into the oncoming storm, the clouds sank into the horizon. He heard a roar of thunder as if it warned of the danger that surrounded him. A couple of seconds elapsed, and more lightning appeared—only this time it was electric blue. The lightning shifted and changed colors with every bolt that occurred. He moved forward as the next strike flashed neon green, and the clouds continually disappeared into the earth. The sky was becoming increasingly darker. He drove toward the light show and saw a yellow flash as the clouds sank further. The thunder roared to life above his head like the sound of the king of the jungle announcing his mating call. A flash of vivid orange struck just twenty feet away from him as the clouds continued to drop. He tried to stop the brute from its journey, but the power of the road pulled him along. Five feet closer to the spot where the last strike hit, he saw the sky open up and the lightning came at him. This time, it burned bright red—the color of blood that dripped from a deep cut.

"Hey, sleeping beauty, wake up."

Drake suddenly jerked awake just before the lightning strike hit him. He looked around; his eyes were blurry from his deep sleep. The boss stared at him and hit Drake's foot to wake him from his snooze in the recliner.

Just over six feet tall, the boss stood before Drake with a smirk on his face and peered at him with his piercing blue eyes; his blond, almost white, hair was spiked. His usually pale features indicated he had spent some time in the sun recently. He still had that innocent boy-next-door look, but he was anything but innocent.

"What? I thought you weren't going to be here until later tonight."

"What time do you think it is? By the way, the sleep didn't improve your looks any. You are still as ugly as the last time I saw you."

"Thanks." Sitting up in the recliner, Drake rubbed the sleep out of his eyes to further wake from the nap. The boss stood in the living room shaking his head. Drake looked at his watch and realized it was 6:00 p.m. "You're still early."

"I wanted to find out if you finished the job I gave you and if there were any problems. What about the other job we talked about?"

"Yeah, I finished the job without any problems. I got rid of the garbage like you asked. That's why they call me Mr. Reliable. I'm waiting to hear about something that I had arranged. Now where's my cash?"

"You are in such a rush to get paid. I don't have the cash on me tonight. I will get it for you tomorrow. Anyway, I thought we could celebrate tonight. I brought some Crown Royal, dinner, and something special if you're interested."

"How come you're in such a good mood?"

"Not in a good mood, just wanted to say thanks for all your hard work. We need to talk about some other things. And before you ask, I will pay you half up front and the other half when you are done, I know the drill."

"Before we get started, I need to clear my head." Drake stood up and stretched and yawned, still groggy from the nap. *Man, I really zonked out,* he thought. As he wondered what the dream meant, it faded as dreams tend to do. The aroma of Chinese food made him realize he was hungry.

He walked into the kitchen, grabbed some plates and glasses from the cupboard, and set them on the table. After grabbing two sets of knives, forks, and extra spoons, he reached for the bag of ice from the freezer. With one hand, he dropped a couple of ice cubes in two glasses and grabbed the fresh bottle of Crown Royal in the other hand and poured the liquor into the glasses. He took a swig. It burned all the way down but felt good. He picked up the other drink and started to make his way into the living room. The boss stood in the doorway that led from the kitchen to the living room, staring off into space.

"Here you go," Drake said as he handed the drink to the boss and added, "Thanks for the food and the drinks. I'm hungry, let's dig in." Sitting opposite one another, Drake removed the cartons from the generic brown bag and placed the food between them. They helped themselves and ate in silence.

Once they had finished eating, the boss asked, "So how have things been?"

"Things are fine; I missed your pleasant arrogance."

"Now look who's being sarcastic. So do you want to hear about my trip?"

"You won't be boring me with all the gory details, will you?" The boss man frowned at Drake, who quickly added, "All right, go ahead."

"The trip was productive. I met some new contacts. They might head out this way for a visit to see what the customers are like."

"Do you think that's a good idea?"

"Why not?"

"People in the community might get suspicious when they see new faces," Drake replied knowingly. "People like to gossip and are curious to know what's going on and who the people are, especially that bitch who doesn't live too far away."

"We won't meet them here but maybe in Edmonton or Calgary. I don't want to let anyone know where we're staying. By the way, I'm not sure if you'll be involved in this meeting."

"What's up with that?" Drake asked. "You're the one who reminds me of appearances and you always want me to tag along. You don't trust me?"

"This has nothing to do with trust. I have something else for you to do."

Chapter Four

Drake stood up from the table and asked, "Hey, boss, you want another?"

"Sure."

Drake turned from the table and walked to the counter for more whiskey. "Thanks again for the dinner, it was rather tasty since I didn't have to pay."

"No problem. Has anything new happened since I've been gone?"

"No. Why do you ask?"

"Just curious, I wanted to find out about the neighbors, especially the nosy one."

"No issues with anyone, and I haven't seen her for a couple of days. Why are you so interested in that neighbor, does she get you hot and bothered?" Drake asked.

The man didn't answer the question, but asked, "Don't you like the way she looks?"

"I wasn't the one asking about her."

"She's good to look at and has a decent body. I wonder what she would be like in the sack."

Drake finished pouring the drink, turned, and handed the glass back to the boss. "Down the hatch," he said and gulped his drink in two long swallows. He looked at the man. "Why don't you go find out?"

The boss looked at Drake with a grin on his face. As Drake turned back to the counter and poured himself another drink, the boss replied with a laugh, "You just never know. I might do that."

Drake shook his head. *The man must have read my mind. Earlier in the day, I thought the same thing but wouldn't admit it.* He downed the drink in his hand. This time, the burning sensation was a little less painful. "You really want to get laid that badly?"

"Not really. I wanted to see your reaction. I didn't know you cared who I slept with."

"I don't. I wouldn't want to mess with that woman. You know she's the type of person that will cause trouble for us."

"I know. I'm just pulling your leg, not to worry. Do you think I would waste my time and effort on her? There are other women more appealing to me. Do you remember the redhead that used to live not too far from here? She lived with her aunt and uncle and a twin sister. The twin was quiet and a little on the chunky side, her name was Mary. Krisi, yeah, that was the other twin's name. Man, she was hot. The sisters moved to Calgary for awhile until Krisi moved to the United States with a hoodlum, who just happened to be an enemy of mine. I had first dibs, though. She returned to Calgary and stayed with Mary for awhile."

Drake poured himself another drink. Each drink seemed a lot smoother to swallow. *Can't let this booze go to waste.* "I remember, what happened to her?"

"Last I heard she was a cold case. No body was found."

"Why have you brought this up now?"

"Well, this is part of what I need you to do for me," Drake's boss replied. "Frighten Mary so she will move back to this neck of the woods. I need something from her."

"We talked about this plan previously and it is in motion ahead of schedule," Drake responded.

"I like having you around. You know what to do before I ask."

"That's what they call me Mr. Reliable." Drake raised his glass, nodded, and said, "Cheers." He finished his drink while the boss sipped his. "Damn, this is good. Do you want another?"

"I'm good, but you go ahead."

"Don't mind if I do."

Chapter Five

June, the following year

Mary had quite a day. *Some people can be so stupid. Why do people have to drive like maniacs or not pay attention?* She should have known better than to travel Deerfoot Trail, which was also known as lead-foot lane. The city was doing road construction, which slowed the traffic to a crawl.

A driver talking on his cell phone didn't watch where he was going. The moron almost ran into her. Another driver, a woman this time, pulled over on the side of the road and suddenly decided to pull out without paying attention to what was beside her. *The bimbo almost caused an accident,* she thought. It was a good thing no one was in the other lane, which allowed Mary to change lanes quickly to avoid getting hit.

Mary parked her Hyundai Tucson in the stall and turned off the ignition. She lowered her head to the steering wheel and took a deep breath and slowly released the air. She did this a second time—glad she had made it back safely and could forget about the loser drivers for now. She was glad her son, Jordie, hadn't been in the SUV with her. After she calmed down, she lifted her head and grabbed her keys, purse, and the bags that had accumulated from her shopping trip.

After she got out of the SUV and locked the doors with the fob that controlled the automatic door locks, she headed to the front door where the mailbox hung on the left. She lifted the mailbox lid and checked inside. She quickly went through the envelopes to see what treasures awaited her—lovely bills, a discount card for glasses from Shopper's Optical, and a letter from a lawyer's office in Three Hills. She placed this envelope on top and would take a closer look at it when she got in the house. She reached for the doorknob but noticed the door was ajar. Before she left to do her errands, she had closed and locked the door. She nudged the door open with her right foot. "What the . . . ."

Chapter Six

Mary stood at the door of her house and saw chaos in the living room. The furniture had been tipped over and slashed, lamps were broken, and pictures had been thrown against the wall and laid face down on the floor with pieces of glass scattered. Before she had left to do her errands, she had finished the housecleaning and everything had been spotless.

Confused, Mary backed up quickly and almost tripped. She rushed to her Tucson and unlocked the doors with the key fob she still clutched in her hand. She grabbed the door handle, which slipped through her fingers as she dropped everything. Mary grabbed the door handle again; this time it opened. She quickly picked up her purse, shopping bags, and mail, then tossed everything onto the passenger seat.

Once she was in her vehicle, she relocked the doors and opened her purse to find her BlackBerry with headset attached. She felt light-headed as she sank into the seat and leaned her head back on the seat's headrest. She closed her eyes for a few moments, waiting for the light-headedness to disappear. She adjusted her hearing aid, put on her headset, and dialed 911. The dial tone rang once, twice, and finally an operator picked up and said, "Police department. What is your emergency?"

"I . . . my house . . . my house . . . has been broken into. I just . . . I don't," she stuttered.

"Are you okay?"

Mary didn't respond. She tried to calm herself by taking a deep cleansing breath and releasing it.

"Ma'am, are you there? Are you okay?"

"I . . . I'm fine but scared," Mary responded in a quivering tone.

"What's your name and where are you?"

"My name . . . my name is Mary and I'm sitting in my SUV, with the doors locked, in front of my house." She gave the operator her address and became aware that her hand holding the BlackBerry was shaking. She inhaled a long breath through her nose and let it escape through her mouth as her shaking subsided.

"A car will be sent shortly. Please stay on the line for a moment while someone's dispatched." Mary was aware of the silence on her BlackBerry as she waited for the operator to return. After a short pause, the operator returned and said, "I will ask you some questions until someone shows up. Did you see anyone?"

"No."

"Where were you before you called in?"

"I was returning from some errands."

"Does anyone live with you?"

"My son, Jordie, he's five."

"Where is he now?"

"He's with a friend of mine."

Mary looked in the rearview mirror and noticed a movement of white with flashing red and blue lights headed in her direction.

The operator said, "There is someone there now, I can hear the siren. I'll hang up, but please remain in your vehicle until the officers tell you that it is okay to get out." The line went dead and the conversation was disconnected.

Mary spotted the police car with two uniformed officers. Both officers stepped out of their patrol car simultaneously with hands on their weapons. One officer, a male, came to Mary's window and pointed one finger at her and then pointed at the SUV and mouthed the word, "Stay."

Mary watched as he turned and walked toward the house and the second officer. The officers approached the front door with their guns drawn. As one officer headed into the house, the other followed directly behind. They passed the foot of the stairs and were soon out of Mary's sight.

While the two officers searched the house, Mary removed her headset. The search seemed to take forever. But in reality, it was only about five minutes before they reappeared at the front door. They returned their guns to their holsters and walked toward her vehicle. The officer who told Mary to stay in her vehicle motioned for her to step out of her SUV. Unlocking and opening the driver's door, she stepped out of her vehicle and walked to the front of it where the two officers joined her.

"Mary?"

She nodded her head yes as she concentrated on the movement of the officer's lips.

"I'm Sergeant Willcox; this is my partner, Officer Smith. We went through your house, but whoever broke in is gone now. We will need our specialists to come and see what they can find, such as fingerprints other than yours, etc. You will not be able to get back into your house today. I know that we received some information from the 911 operator, but we need to ask you more detailed questions that might give us some clues as to what happened."

Willcox paused for a moment and asked, "How are you?"

Mary noticed his smoky gray eyes and answered, "I don't . . . I don't know. I just can't figure out why this happened. What's going on?" Neither officer replied to her question.

"Do you have somewhere you can stay tonight?" asked Willcox.

"Yes, I do, but I'll need to make a phone call. My friend Kath is taking care of Jordie."

Willcox looked at Mary and said, "We'll talk before you make that phone call. We'll be as quick as possible, but we need details of the events that led up to the time that you got home. Before we get started, we'll call for backup and get the process going."

Officer Smith stepped aside for a few moments and talked on her radio for backup. When she returned, Willcox looked at Mary and said, "Step us through what happened from the time you left home until the time you contacted 911."

As Mary described her day, three more officers showed up. She couldn't add anything else to what she had told the 911 operator over the telephone. Finishing her story, she took a deep breath and exhaled.

Smith looked at Mary and touched her arm. "You can make that call now. We need to talk to the others. Please stay here after you've made your phone call."

"Thank you." Mary searched in her purse for the BlackBerry and headset. Before she could make her call, the BlackBerry signaled there was a message. Kath wanted to let her know that she was taking Jordie swimming and would send a message once they were done to meet for an early dinner.

After the conversation with the officers, Mary felt shaky. She turned toward her SUV and opened the door to sit in the driver's seat. With the BlackBerry still in her hand, she put her head against the headrest and stared out the window to clear her mind. *Who would break into the house and why? There wasn't much of value to steal.* She looked at the BlackBerry but decided to return Kath's message later.

Chapter Seven

After Mary talked to the officers once more, they told her she could leave. She was still shocked as to why someone would want to break into her house. She had very little of value to take. *What the heck was going on?* She wanted to go for a drive and knew there was time. It had only been twenty minutes since Kath had sent her a text message. She thought of the one place she could go that would calm her.

On her way to that special place, Mary was lost in her own thoughts and didn't notice the vehicle that followed her from a safe distance. After moving to the city with her sister Krisi, they had often met at the park to talk and have picnics.

Now, she pulled into the parking area, grabbed her purse, stepped out of the SUV, and locked the doors. She took a deep breath and started out on the five-minute walk to the picnic area. The gravel path curved past the swings, slide, and monkey bars then continued through a gate onto a hiker's path that led to the picnic area with tables and fire pits. *This park is great. I should bring Jordie here,* she thought. She remembered the great times when she and Krisi had packed a lunch and just talked about things and spent time together.

Mary walked to their favorite table. She looked down at the end of the table and smiled when she saw their initials carved in the corner. Sitting on top of the table, she traced her finger across the wood and felt the indentation made by their initials and wished her sister was sitting beside her.

Mary reflected on the times when they were in elementary school. Krisi was always the loud, boisterous one while Mary was the quiet one. Krisi was such a tomboy. When she was four or five, she always wanted to play with hot wheels instead of dolls. Mary suddenly remembered Krisi's favorite car. It was a red sports car with the decal of glowing red, yellow, and orange flames along both sides. She wondered what had happened to that little car.

In grade eight, Mary developed a crush on a boy in her class named Kenny. He and his friends found out and began to tease her about it steadily and thought it was a big joke. Mary was heartbroken when the thoughts of having a boyfriend turned into a total fiasco. While the situation seemed to hound Mary forever, it was actually only a week. After that episode, never again did she have feelings for anyone in her class. She really didn't like school at all—especially when most of the kids teased her about her fiery red hair and freckles. Krisi didn't have that many freckles, and her hair was strawberry blonde, a much different shade than Mary's red. That was the time when things started to change between the two of them.

Krisi was always the one who got into trouble at school—especially after grade nine. Her body bloomed with a model's figure at age fifteen. When all the boys suddenly wanted to be Krisi's friend, Mary was jealous of the attention that Krisi received. It was difficult for her to make friends, especially male friends. The sisters were twins but not identical. They were as opposite as black and white. Mary had a different body shape than her sister. She was more bulky and clumsy, not slender and graceful like Krisi. Even their personalities were different. Krisi was outgoing and always full of mischief; Mary was shy and more subdued.

Once they graduated from school and moved into the city, they went their separate ways shortly after. They kept in touch for a while, but the communication dwindled. Mary took university classes at night and worked during the day. Krisi ended up with a man Mary knew nothing about and moved from Calgary to the United States where she was a kept woman, a trophy. Mary had a few male friends but nothing serious, as she was too busy with personal projects.

The sounds of birds chirping turned Mary's thoughts back to the present. *Why would someone break into my house?* She wondered.

There was nothing of value in the house—only a few electronics, no valuable jewelry, and very little money—only change for ice cream when they decided to walk to Dairy Queen. When she had pushed the door open she hadn't paid much attention other than to get back into her SUV and call 911. She was grateful that no one had been at home. *Although,* she thought, *then none of this would have happened.*

Mary remembered the day when Krisi had phoned and asked her to meet at their usual place for lunch the next day. Krisi mentioned that she really needed Mary's help. Mary wanted to see her sister and could not refuse. The day came and Mary went to the park carrying a packed picnic lunch with most of Krisi's favorites, just like old times. Krisi was already at their usual table. She was off in her own dream world with the sun shining on top of her hair. The day was beautiful. Birds chirped their midday songs, a warm breeze blew, and the day was a reminder of the picnics they used to have. The sound of Mary setting the basket on the table startled Krisi. She immediately stood up to give her sister a hug. Mary would never forget that afternoon and the miracle it brought.

"What's up?" Mary questioned Krisi.

"I need a favor, a big favor."

Mary's face turned sour as she thought, *Oh, no, now what?*

Krisi looked at Mary and started to laugh. "I know that look. I've gotten you into some bizarre things, but I really do need your help with this. I'm pregnant. I want you to raise the baby after the delivery as if it was your own. I'm due in about six months. I'll contact a lawyer and ensure the paperwork is ready." Krisi laughed at Mary's stunned expression.

"Why do you want me to do this?"

"I know you would be the better parent. I'm not the type to settle down. A child needs stability and I'm not so good at that. I have to know if you will do what I ask. Abortion is out of the question. Right now, I can't explain any of this."

After a bit more discussion on the topic, Mary relented.

Krisi was a bundle of nerves and told Mary she had to go away for a bit until the baby was born. After the birth, she would contact

Mary. Krisi explained that she did not want to go into the details, but Mary had to promise that she would take care of the baby after Krisi contacted her with the adoption papers. After the picnic lunch, Mary and Krisi went their separate ways.

Before the baby was born, Mary became very ill with Ménière's disease, which causes inner ear damage. She lost her hearing in both ears, had dizzy spells, experienced nausea, and lost weight. Eventually, life returned to normal except she had to wear hearing aids in both ears. Occasionally, she still experienced lightheadedness and dizzy spells, but this was nothing compared to what it used to be like.

Krisi's baby boy, named Jordie, was beautiful. He had bright blue eyes, a full head of strawberry-blond, and a good disposition. Krisi moved in with Mary for awhile just to get reacquainted and help get things settled.

During this time, Mary was diagnosed with a form of breast cancer called ductal carcinoma in situ (DCIS). Over a year and a half, she went through a lot, including a partial and then a full mastectomy and breast reconstruction. Additional testing indicated there was no need for chemotherapy or radiation. So far, every test result gave no indication of cancer recurring or spreading.

Once Mary was out of the woods, Krisi decided it was time to move on. This was a very sad time for Mary. Krisi was Mary's rock—a crutch to lean on when times were tough. For a time, the two women communicated at least twice a week and then the contact decreased. After a few months, it completely stopped.

When Jordie was two, Mary heard a knock on the door. Two detectives gave her bad news about Krisi. There was an indication of murder at the scene and not much evidence to solve the crime. Six months later, boxes were delivered to Mary's house containing Krisi's personal effects.

Mary wouldn't forget the day she received the devastating news that her sister could be dead. Even though they had drifted apart, they had that special connection. Deep inside her body, Mary sensed her sister was alive somewhere.

Chapter Eight

As Mary's thoughts returned to the present, she glanced at the trees in the park and noticed the branches swayed, yet there was no wind. *How could that be?* Suddenly sensing someone was observing her, she turned, but no one was there. A few couples were scattered around at other picnic tables. Enjoying the sunshine, they talked and laughed, but no one paid any attention to her. Yet the nagging feeling of being observed continued.

Mary checked her watch. It was 5:00 p.m. She couldn't believe how long she had sat at the picnic table venturing into her past. She checked her BlackBerry, but there were no messages showing on the screen.

She was glad Jordie hadn't been with her when she got home from her errands. She still couldn't figure out what was going on. *Why would anyone want to break into our home? Did they want to steal something? Was there something else?*

Mary shivered as a cool breeze came up and swept over her as a dark cloud covered the sun's warmth. She glanced where she had seen the movement earlier. Now there was only stillness, but she continued to sense someone was lurking among the trees.

For a few years, sadness had surrounded her life. Her aunt and uncle, who lived at the farm that her parents had owned, were like a second set of parents. They both passed away shortly after Krisi was supposedly murdered.

Health-wise, she had never felt better. But a recurring thought crept in the back of her mind that the cancer was going to return. It was like a worm that kept burrowing deeper. When she had learned she couldn't conceive, she felt empty. At least Jordie was the one highlight in her life, and she had to be strong for him. Things happened in life and she knew she had to deal with it the best she could. Being upset did little to help, and it wasn't good for the blood pressure.

The BlackBerry vibrated in Mary's hand. She had a message from Kath. They had just left the pool and headed to the library. She would send another message when they were finished so they could meet for dinner.

Well, enough of the past, Mary sighed. She couldn't change anything and had to move on. Maybe she was ready for some changes. For now, she needed to get back to the SUV and wait for Kath's message. Mary got up from the table and took one last look at where she had seen the branches moving. Even with a gentle breeze now, everything was still. Nothing out of the ordinary suggested anything lurking in the shadows. Maybe it was just her imagination about the branches. Although it was quiet, Mary continued to sense a presence.

As she headed back to her Tucson, taking the same pathway she used to reach the picnic area, her BlackBerry vibrated. This time, Kath was letting her know that they were leaving the library and heading to Montana's for dinner.

Mary opened her SUV door, slipped in the driver's seat, and relocked it. She took a moment to reply to Kath's text. She let her know she would be at the restaurant in twenty minutes and to go ahead and get a table. Before leaving the parking lot, Mary glanced around once more but didn't notice anything strange. She backed out of her parking spot and drove toward the exit. She wasn't in the mood to eat.

On the way to the restaurant, a vehicle tailed Mary's SUV. The driver kept enough of a distance between the vehicles so no one would be suspicious. His car was nondescript and nothing out of the ordinary.

Traffic was light, and Mary made it to the restaurant ahead of schedule. She was pleased to notice Kath's car was already in the lot. She parked her SUV, exited, and locked the door. As Mary headed toward the restaurant, she suddenly stopped. She scanned the parking lot to see if there was anyone watching. No one. She headed for the door.

*   *   *

The vehicle that had followed Mary's SUV earlier now appeared as Mary entered the restaurant. The vehicle stopped and parked. Ned, Drake's sidekick, got out of his vehicle and headed in the direction of his target's parking spot. Dropping his keys next to the car, he reached into his jacket pocket and pulled out a small, magnetized, metal box. He squatted down to retrieve the dropped keys and quickly attached the small box on the underside of the driver's side. Once the task was complete, he stood up, turned back toward his vehicle, and left the unattended vehicle as if nothing had happened.

Chapter Nine

Mary entered the restaurant and scanned the crowd as she looked for Jordie and Kath. She walked to the left, but they weren't at any of the tables. She moved to the right and noticed Kath in the back corner waving to get Mary's attention. Mary walked to the corner booth where the two were seated. Jordie concentrated on his coloring and didn't notice Mary slide into the seat.

Kath looked at Mary's glum face hidden behind a fake smile. Jordie glanced up to look at Mary with a wide smile on his face. "Hi, Momma."

"Hey, sweetie, how was your day?"

"It was great. We went to the park, swimming, and then the place with all the books."

"You mean the library?"

"Yeah, that's it. Auntie got some for me to look at later."

"So what are you coloring?"

"A surprise; can't have it until I'm done." Once again, Jordie was busy with his picture.

"A surprise for me, I can hardly wait."

Kath looked at Mary and asked, "What's up?"

"Kath, I have a favor. Could we spend the night at your house?"

"Of course, can I ask you why?"

"I'll explain later. Right now isn't a good time. I really appreciate that we can stay with you. It will give us some time to get caught up, and I can tell you what happened today."

"Okay. Since we have time, let's have a movie night with snacks. What do you think, Jordie?"

Jordie looked up at Kath and replied, "Yippee! We get to watch a movie. Can we get *Happy Feet?*"

"Well, when we go to the video store we will see what they have. If they have it, we can rent it."

"Okay." Jordie returned to his coloring.

The waitress appeared, took Mary's drink order, and their food order. They talked about anything but what occurred during the day. Twenty minutes later, the food arrived. Hungry, everyone ate in silence. Now that he was fed, Jordie was ready to get the movie and head to Kath's. Kath placed the tip on the table and paid the bill. As they walked out of the restaurant, Mary suggested that she and Jordie would pick up the movies and snacks and meet Kath at her house.

They enjoyed *Happy Feet* and ate popcorn. Jordie fell asleep on the floor cuddled up in a sleeping bag. Kath turned off the DVD player so she and Mary could talk quietly. Mary explained the day's events as Kath listened with a shocked expression but didn't interrupt Mary. She was about to ask Mary questions when Mary's cell phone vibrated to indicate a call was coming through. She picked it up and said, "Hello."

"Hi Mary, this is Sergeant Willcox."

"Sergeant Willcox, how are you?"

"I'm fine. Could you please meet us at your house around 10:00 a.m. tomorrow?"

"Is there something wrong?"

"We need to ask you a few more questions. You said you never went inside after pushing the door open. We'd like to determine if anything was taken from your house. We would really appreciate your time in this matter."

"Will I be able to get back into my house tomorrow?"

"We can discuss this further tomorrow. You had quite a day. Get some rest, and we'll see you in the morning."

"All right, have a good evening."

"You too, Mary, take care."

Mary hung up the phone and looked at Kath. "It was nice of him to phone, but I have a feeling something is wrong. He avoided answering my questions."

"What did he say?"

Mary explained the conversation and when she would meet the officers.

"Okay, why don't we have some wine and try to relax like he said. We have our movie to watch. Wait and see what tomorrow brings. Maybe he just wants to see you again."

Mary smiled and rolled her eyes and said, "You make me laugh." She realized he was kind of cute but thought that he was probably already taken.

As the smell of popcorn lingered in the air, Kath smiled and got up to get their drinks. Mary mulled over what was going on but had no answers to all the questions that popped into her head like kernels of popcorn being toasted. She would have to wait until tomorrow to find out what was up. No use stressing about it until it happened. A glass of wine or two sounded good.

Chapter Ten

The sun peeked through the slit in the drapes. The smell of bacon sizzled in the air. The aroma of coffee filled her nostrils. Even though she liked the scent, she no longer drank the brew. Mary slowly opened her eyes and glanced around the room. None of her familiar belongings were anywhere to be found. It finally dawned on her that she wasn't dreaming. This was real, it happened. She popped in her hearing aid and heard the faint hum of distant conversation but couldn't understand what was being said. Jordie laughed. He was such a sweetie and, miraculously, he was a part of her life.

Her sleep had been continuously disrupted as her bad dream kept waking her. She dreamed of the break-in and that the two of them were at home when it occurred. She glanced at the alarm clock on the nightstand and the numbers illuminated 8:00 a.m. She stretched her arms over her head and let out a big yawn. She was scheduled to meet with the officers at 10:00 a.m., which gave her a couple of hours to get ready. She got up and made the bed. On her way to the bathroom, she grabbed a couple of towels from the linen closet. She removed her hearing aid and hoped the shower would wake her up, as her brain was clogged. Mornings with the lack of sleep were the hardest days to get motivated.

After the water warmed up, she stepped into the shower and thought of the previous day—the break-in and, of course, Sergeant Willcox. He was easy on the eyes and very nice to her. His unique, smoky gray eyes were unforgettable. At least, she could see the real man soon. She had to stop fantasizing of Willcox and concentrate on what the day was about to bring. Still, he could be her arm candy anytime.

She shut off the water, stepped out of the shower, and retrieved her towels. She wrapped her wet hair and body so she could make her way back to the bedroom and get dressed in the clothes that Kath had thoughtfully laundered last night.

Before she left the bathroom, she noticed someone had slid a note underneath the door. It stated that breakfast would be ready in ten minutes. She smiled and dressed quickly; the smell of pancakes cooking made her stomach grumble. After she was dressed, combed, and the hearing aids were popped in again, she made her way to the kitchen. Jordie ran up to her, and she knelt down to get a hug.

"What have you been up to this morning, Jordie?"

"Auntie and I made breakfast. Now it's ready. Come on, let's eat."

He unwrapped himself from her grasp, and she gave him a kiss on the forehead.

"Well, it smells wonderful, you did a fine job. Love you, Pooh."

"Love you, Momma."

She stood up. Jordie grabbed her hand and led the way to the table, which was already set with breakfast ready to be eaten.

"Kath, you shouldn't have gone to so much trouble."

"No trouble, Jordie said he was hungry, wanted pancakes, and could eat a bear." Kath acted like she was a bear ready to attack him. Jordie giggled.

"I'm going to eat the bear before she eats me."

"By the way, Sergeant Willcox phoned while you were in the shower and asked if you could come alone this morning. You haven't got much time, so eat up."

"Okay, that makes sense." Mary was disturbed by the request but it was probably for the best. "Do you mind if Jordie stays with you while I'm out?"

"No problem. No need to ask. So Jordie, what would you like to do while your mom's away?"

"Birthday party, yippee."

Mary looked at Jordie, who had stuffed his face with pancakes, and then at Kath. "What day is it today?"

"It's Saturday the third."

"Oh, crap. I forgot. That was one of the reasons I went shopping yesterday. I got a gift, but it's still in the SUV. The past twenty-four hours has been something else, it totally slipped my mind. Susie's birthday party is at Chucky Cheese around one for lunch and activities. Kath, do you mind taking him to the party?"

"What do you think, Jordie? Do you want me to take you to the party?"

"Yup," Jordie said as he managed to stuff in another mouthful of pancakes.

"Jordie, you know better. It is 'Yes, please,' and slow down with the breakfast. You're going to choke," Mary said with an amused sigh.

"Sorry, Momma. Yes, Auntie, I would like you to take me to the party, please."

"Then it's settled," Kath said with a smile. "Eat your breakfast and meet the officers at your house. Remember to give me the gift, so we can get it ready for the party."

The rest of the breakfast went by without a hitch. Mary enjoyed the chatter and laughter. Still, in the back of her mind, she was sure something was going on at her house that eluded her.

Chapter Eleven

Drake woke up and looked at the clock perched on the nightstand. It read 10:30 a.m. His mouth was dry, and he needed water. The sound of silence prevailed except for the clock ticking. *Maybe the boss left and won't be back,* he wondered. *Could I be so lucky?*

He moved his long, lanky legs over to the side of the bed as he stretched, yawned, and rubbed the haziness from his eyes. The drapes were closed, but the sun beamed through the gaps, hinting the day was going to be hot. As he stood up, his brain tried to register what had occurred the previous night. The boss showed up, brought dinner, Crown Royal, and some wonderful weed that hit the spot. Man that was a great hit. After all that, everything went fuzzy. He stepped over to the dresser and grabbed a pair of khaki shorts and pulled them on. His mouth was dry and felt like it was stuffed full of cotton. He was starved, but he had to take a leak first. He opened the bedroom door and noticed all the other doors were open. He made a side trip to the bathroom before heading to the kitchen.

The boss was gone. Drake went to the kitchen to get a bottle of water from the refrigerator. He unscrewed the cap and took several gulps. So refreshing. When he turned around, he saw a note on the table. He picked it up and read it.

"I went to get some money from a customer and food for the house. I left at 10:00 and should be back in a few hours. You sure had a great time last night and were quite the comedian. Cheers."

Drake looked at the water bottle that was now three-quarters empty. He finished the rest in one long swallow. *What did the boss mean by his comment? Very strange. Oh well, at least there was laughter.*

His stomach grumbled. He left the empty bottle on the table and returned to the fridge to get the fixings for a sandwich. He placed everything on the counter then grabbed another bottle of water, opened it, and chugged half of it down. Drake made himself a ham and cheese sandwich. *I should've known better than to drink so much hard liquor,* he thought. *But then, what fun would that be? At least I never get hangovers. Now, what was I about to do? Oh yeah, the sandwich.*

The fogginess cleared somewhat, but he still couldn't remember much of what had happened last night. The boss would probably remind him later. He had time for a shower and would be ready for whatever the boss tossed his way. He hoped the man would stay away for a little while longer. He wasn't quite ready to deal with that jerk yet.

*   *   *

The boss man sat in Tim Horton's enjoying an extra-large black coffee and checking out the foxy ladies with their short shorts. Some were hot, some were not, and there was a whole lot of jailbait. He enjoyed the warm, summery days. When there was heat, the ladies tended to dress light to stay cool.

Lately, his thoughts drifted to the times that he had spent with Krisi. She was a spitfire and knew what turned him on. She was the only person that understood how he ticked and always knew when something bothered him. She had a way of getting him to open up to her.

He wanted to find out what had happened to her and what it was that she had kept from him. He couldn't figure out what it was or why she left him for the one person he couldn't stand, his archrival. He had been out of the country at the time when this happened.

For a while, he had searched for her, but it was as though she had disappeared off the face of the earth. With no luck finding her, he continued on with his life. He pretended she never existed. But most of the time it was hard to do, as he kept thinking about her. He needed to know the secret that she had never revealed to him. One way or another, he was going to find out what it was.

The plan was in motion for her sister, Mary, to move back to the family home where they grew up. He had to think of a way to get close to Mary. He hoped the two sisters would be a lot more alike now that Mary was older.

He needed Drake to search the property to determine if anything of Krisi's was left behind.

Let the games begin.

Chapter Twelve

Breakfast was finished. Mary said good-bye, walked to her SUV for the drive to her house for her appointment. Again, she experienced the uneasy feeling of being watched. She stopped as she reached for the door handle on the SUV and scanned the area to see whether anyone was hanging around that looked unfamiliar, but she didn't see anyone. With the SUV doors unlocked, she slid into the driver's seat and relocked the doors. She sat there for a moment. She took a deep breath and let the air escape from her lungs. Then she hooked the seat belt, started the engine, and backed out of the stall to drive to her house.

Traffic was light, and she made it in plenty of time. She pulled up in front of her house and noticed the yellow crime scene tape that stated DO NOT CROSS in bold, black letters and was stretched across the front door. She found this a bit odd. *Was there anything out of the ordinary other than someone that broke into her house?* She checked her watch; it was 10:00 a.m. She looked up and noticed a plain, white car pull in behind hers. Two people sat in front. As Mary got out of her vehicle, so did the two officers she had met the previous day. They strolled toward her.

"Hi, Mary," Sergeant Willcox said with a soft, concerned look on his face. "How are you doing today?"

Mary looked at his mouth, his smoky gray eyes, and kept thinking to herself, *Wow*. She was dumbfounded. He seemed serious but friendly. "Well, I'm not so sure."

"Why?"

"I've been on pins and needles since yesterday about this. I can't figure out why this happened or who would've done such a thing."

34

Willcox and Smith quickly exchanged a glance.

"Okay, Mary. Now, let's go inside and you can see for yourself. I didn't want to mention any of this yesterday or over the phone last night, but there are some disturbing scenes."

Mary didn't respond, but looked at Willcox with a puzzled expression on her face. He turned and moved away from her before she had the chance to ask any questions. The three walked toward the house in silence. Willcox was in the lead, Mary second, and then Smith. They made their way up the three steps as he pushed the tape aside, opened the door, and stepped inside. He turned toward Mary before she took a step forward to enter. "Are you ready?" he asked and looked into her eyes for any unspoken answer.

"As ready as I'll ever be." Mary had barely crossed the threshold when she first noticed the dark blue words printed on the walls. Don't stay here. You will suffer if you do. It looked like a graffiti artist used spray-paint to leave his mark.

A mixture of blue and red paints had been used. Often the red stood alone. The red was the color of a beautiful red rose but what she saw was a warning. On the opposite wall, more words with jagged letters screamed: the bitch is dead, now it's your turn. The words were deadly.

A couple of pictures hung on the walls. One was of Krisi with a large X drawn through it. The other photo was of Mary and Jordie taken in Wal-Mart's photography department. A question mark was scribbled on Mary's face. Both pictures were removed from their frames and stuck to the wall with small daggers in each of the corners with something dripping from the handle.

Mary took a step back and almost toppled over Smith, who stood directly behind her. Smith grabbed Mary's arm to steady her. Willcox turned toward the two women to see what had happened. He quickly grabbed Mary's other arm to keep her upright and helped her to a chair.

Feeling lightheaded, Mary put her head between her legs and took deep breaths to calm down. Willcox and Smith released their hold on her arms. Mary watched as they retreated to the entryway for privacy and to talk quietly. Mary thought that was funny but didn't laugh. She wouldn't have been able to hear their conversation anyhow.

After a few minutes, Mary had calmed down and the lightheadedness abated. She faced the full view of the damaged pictures and felt a tear gently slide down her cheek. With her right hand, she quickly wiped it away.

The officers returned and Willcox stood in front of Mary, blocking the view of the pictures that disturbed her. "How are you doing, Mary?"

Mary looked at the mouth of the man she was so attracted to and then looked into his gray eyes. "I'm just peachy."

"There is more to see if you're ready."

"Can you please tell me if there is anything worse than this?"

"Not sure if this is the worst. I know you must be scared. There is more paint, writings on the walls, and something else."

Smith came close to Mary and bent down on her knees to be at Mary's level. "I will take your arm, and we will walk through this mess together. Lean on me, okay?"

"All right, I guess." Mary wasn't all right about anything, but she needed to see what had happened to her safe haven—only it wasn't that anymore.

Mary felt that Jordie and she wouldn't be safe in this environment. She sighed and felt something cold slide down her spine, and shivered as if someone or something had just walked over her grave.

She turned her head as she felt the reassuring pressure of Smith's hand on her arm. "Spooky in here, isn't it? It's probably your nerves playing tricks on you. Ready?"

Mary nodded slightly.

Smith took Mary's arm and helped her get up from the chair. Both women walked to the kitchen and passed through the door archway. As Mary passed the wall with the pictures, it seemed to pulsate. She quickly turned away, took a deep breath, and forced herself to look at the kitchen. The cupboards were open and the contents were scattered on the floor. A few doors were damaged beyond repair. Every door hung open. Blue paint on all four walls made a design that seemed familiar, but she couldn't quite place it. The door to the pantry stood partially open and she saw a shadow. More words appeared: DANGER IS PENDING.

She jumped slightly as Smith pressed her arm. Smith said, "It's all right, we're here with you."

Willcox glanced at the back window, not observing her or the surroundings. The women returned their attention to the pantry. Slowly, they walked toward it. Mary nudged the door open wide with her foot. She saw a paper model of what looked like her sister. Around the neck, a rope hung from the ceiling. The tongue stuck out from grotesque facial features. The contents of the pantry spread beneath the model's feet. A note attached to the arm stated: "The bitch is dead, you're next." Mary gasped as Smith tightened her grip on Mary's arm. Mary moved away from the scene and Smith followed.

"What's going on? Who would do such a thing?" Mary asked as she looked at Smith and then Willcox. She knew neither one of them had an answer.

Willcox looked at Mary and gently said, "We need you to look at something upstairs. It isn't much better than this. We want to know if the message has any meaning to you. I know you're upset, but we need your help. Okay?"

Oh man, I'm not ready for anything, Mary thought. She felt a reassuring pressure on her arm from Smith. Mary looked at her and back at Willcox. His gray eyes looked so comforting; his face showed concern. She knew she had to see what was upstairs. "All right, let's get this over with. I don't want to be in this house much longer. I can't stay here anymore."

"You don't have to decide that right now. Take a few days to think about it. Your insurance company will get someone in here to clean up the mess and make repairs," Smith said.

The three of them made their way out of the kitchen into the living room and headed for the stairs. Mary turned and glanced at the pictures. Her mind played tricks on her as she noticed the walls still pulsated. She quickly turned away and moved toward the stairs. Willcox began to climb up. Mary, supported by Smith, managed the steps even though it was a tight fit for the two women. Willcox moved aside so Mary could see Jordie's room.

Yellow paint was smeared over the blue and white decals of race cars and dinosaurs on the walls. The dresser drawers were ransacked. The contents were dumped askew on the floor and tossed across the room. The bedding was shredded, there was a long metal sword standing upright in the centre of the mattress. The lamp on the nightstand was smashed into small pieces. Mary looked in another direction. She thought, *Why would anyone want to do this?* Jordie's toys were damaged; his stuffed animals were all torn apart. Some were positioned face up with long, fine cuts in their necks and what looked like blood that oozed out of the slits. Mary walked away from the remains of the room that her son had once slept in.

She walked to the door of the bathroom. All of the contents were scattered on the floor and in the bathtub. She looked at the bathroom mirror and noticed the red paint in another strange pattern. It too seemed familiar, but she couldn't remember where she had seen it before.

One final room to look at. Willcox entered her bedroom and Mary followed close behind him. She frowned and shook her head. Could anything be salvaged? All her clothes were torn, ripped, and splashed with paint. When she turned and walked away from the closet, she noticed her bedding was ripped and the mattress was upturned. She noticed a dried spot on the box spring—she didn't want to know what it was. The walls were punctured as though a boxer had practiced his shots. Red paint was everywhere—the walls, carpet, and bedroom furniture. The pillows had been tossed on the floor and sliced open. The stuffing scattered like confetti tossed at a wedding. Willcox and Smith stood side by side; Mary sensed she hadn't seen the worst yet.

Willcox said, "Mary, we're going to stand next to you and ask you to look at something. Tell us if it means anything to you."

Mary looked at Willcox and then Smith. She just stared at them. She didn't want to see what lurked behind them but knew she had to.

They both stepped aside and Mary gasped. "Oh, my . . . ," she cried out and slowly sank to the floor.

*   *   *

Drake's "assistant" Ned parked a block away from the house and chuckled. *It was a good idea,* he thought, *to bug the place to hear what was going on.* He wanted to know what happened when Mary got a good look at all the surprises he left for her and wondered what she thought of them. The boss would be extremely grateful for all his hard work. His imagination was a good thing. Hopefully, she would get the hint and move away.

Chapter Thirteen

Drake had just stepped out of the shower when his cell phone rang. Damn, where's the phone? He was expecting an important call. Quickly wrapping a towel around his waist, he headed into the living room. In a rush, he nearly tripped over the area rug. As he caught his balance by grabbing the armrest of the couch, he saw his phone on the end table. He snatched it up, and answered with a breathless "Hello."

Ned responded, "I wasn't able to find the decorations for the party in the house, but the party has started. You should get your present soon; I will let you know when it's sent. The preparations are complete." Drake listened to dead silence as the caller hung up.

The second part was awesome news. At least there was something decent to tell the boss when he got back and, hopefully, he would be pleased.

Drake trudged back to the bathroom and patted his recently shaved head dry. He thought the look made him look tougher. Maybe now the associates wouldn't focus on his youthful appearance. His looks were deceiving. Most of the time, it worked to his advantage. The boss was a fool, but some of his suggestions were good. This time, the boss was right; the change was a good one. Drake dressed in jeans and a T-shirt and waited for the boss to appear. His mind had cleared from the effects of the drinking and weed that he had enjoyed the previous night.

On his way to the kitchen to get a bottle of water, he heard the sound of an engine of a truck pull into the yard. He glanced out the window to determine who it was. He wasn't in the mood for idle chatter with one of the neighbors. It was past lunch time. As though on cue, his stomach growled. Good timing; the boss had showed up.

His boss lifted the truck's box cover and retrieved the groceries. Drake headed to the front door and opened it. As the boss walked through with his arms laden with bags, Drake greeted him, "Hey boss, what's shaking?"

"Sleeping beauty finally woke up. Did your Prince Charming give you a kiss?" Drake rolled his eyes in response. "Don't just stand there; help me with the rest of the bags," ordered the boss.

Drake shook his head and smirked. "Now you're the one who's the comedian. I can see that you had a successful trip. You're asking a lot, but hang on and let me put on my shoes."

"You want to eat, don't you? I also brought you a gift. I will give it to you when we're done. By the way, it was successful."

They brought the last of the groceries inside. Silence hung in the air as they put them away. Once the task was completed, the boss whistled at Drake and tossed him a sub from Subway. "Here's lunch."

"Thanks, man. I'll grab a couple of beers and give you some news after we eat." They sat at the table to chow down on their lunch. "Aah, this hit the spot," Drake said. "Now here's the news. While you were out, I got a phone call. Mary's place was broken into with more than a few surprises left for her. Now, we wait for her to arrive in this neck of the woods. Ned couldn't find what he was looking for in the house. The information isn't there."

"I hope Ned was good and that we won't have any issues. By the way, that's great news except for the information not being found. Sounds like things are moving along." The boss dug in his pocket and pulled out a wad of cash. He separated out a handful of bills and tossed them to Drake. Scooping up the cash, Drake started to count the dough. "What, you don't trust me?" the boss asked.

"You taught me the hard way not to trust anyone and that included you, especially when money was involved."

"You know I wouldn't screw you around. You're the best." Drake gave the man a look but continued counting. "By the way, Drake, there is a bonus in there for you."

Drake verified his payment and began to smile. "Thank you for the compliment. You are generous, and I truly appreciate the gesture."

"I have to keep my employees happy. If this works out as planned, there will be another bonus for you in the end."

Chapter Fourteen

Mary felt dampness on her face and slowly opened her eyes. She saw Smith and assumed she must have been responsible for the cool washcloth on her forehead. She took a breath and slowly released it.

Smith gently asked, "Mary, are you all right?"

Mary closed her eyes again and reopened them as she realized what had just happened. "How long have I been out? What? I can't believe it. Who is that?" She slowly sat up with the help from Smith.

"You have been out for a couple of minutes. Who does it look like?"

"From what I saw, even though briefly, she looks a lot like me but the hair is different."

Willcox piped in, "The good news is that it is not a real person, the body is a dummy."

Mary gave him a critical look and added, "Is that supposed to make me feel better? Okay, maybe a little. Why would someone do this to me?" She felt the tears welling up, but she knew she had to keep from breaking down. She just wanted to get out of there.

Willcox kneeled down to Mary's level. He looked at her apologetically and squeezed her arm. "Mary, I don't know what to say about any of this, but you're doing great. This is one sick bas . . . man. We'll do everything we can to find him and make sure he gets charged with what he's done. There is just one other thing we need you to look at before we leave. We really need your help."

Mary turned away from Willcox and looked toward the dummy that she had seen minutes ago. For all she knew, it could have been an hour. She turned to face Willcox and sighed, "What is it? How can I help? I apologize. I shouldn't have snapped at you. I just don't . . . ." Mary couldn't finish what she wanted to say. She put her head in her hands, moved her knees to her chest, and closed her eyes. Willcox gently rubbed her shoulder. She knew she couldn't let herself get upset, she had to be strong. She took a couple of minutes to take some deep breaths and exhale. At least she didn't cry, which was a good sign. Mary remained on the floor. Finally, she brought her hands away from her face. *Who would do this? Why me? What's going on? This is just total crap.* Willcox took his hand away and moved aside.

Mary felt drained and hot. She looked pale and knew she couldn't stay much longer. Smith held out her arm to help her stand up. Smith tightened her grip on Mary's arm and said, "It's okay, I'm not going anywhere."

Mary noticed that Willcox had turned the dummy over. She couldn't believe what she saw. Where the face should have been, it was blank. There were no outlines of facial features of any kind. The hair was a deep red—almost the same shade as when she was a young girl. Her eyes trailed down to the chest area where a piece of yellow paper was attached to the human form with what looked like two nails. Her eyes raced to the bold, block letters printed on the top of the paper. THIS COULD HAVE BEEN YOU. YOU WERE LUCKY NOT TO HAVE BEEN HOME.

Mary jerked her arm from Smith's hold and fled the bedroom. The walls of the house seemed to slowly invade her space. She had to get out before they closed in on her. In her rush down the stairs, she almost missed the last two steps but was quick to get her balance as she ran out the front door. Momentarily she felt sick, but the feeling subsided once she was in the fresh air.

Outside, she felt exposed and that something was lurking but didn't know where it was. She scanned the area without noticing anything out of the ordinary. She desperately wanted to escape from this horror.

* * *

Ned noticed Mary looking around, but she didn't seem to notice him. She didn't look impressed. He had planted listening devices inside the house and had heard the conversations between Mary and the cops. Now they were coming out after her. *Oh, this is much more fun than watching mystery shows on TV,* he thought, and chuckled to himself.

Chapter Fifteen

The hot, muggy day was almost over by the time the two men finished eating and putting the groceries away. "Hey, Drake, I have to leave for a couple of days and should be back on Monday."

Drake couldn't believe what he heard. This day couldn't have turned out any better. He wondered what was up but knew that soon enough he would find out.

"While I'm gone, I want you to look in the farm house and surrounding buildings where Krisi and Mary grew up. See if Krisi left anything behind. The place is empty, but I'm hoping a woman and child will be living there shortly."

"How do you expect me to get on the property without someone noticing?" Drake knew exactly what to do. He just wanted the boss to feel he was smarter.

"Right now, the property is up for sale but not advertised. I'm sure you will think of something. What do you think I pay you for if you can't think of a plan of action on your own?"

"Yeah, yeah, whatever. I'll get the job done with or without your assistance. So where are you going?"

"I have a few meetings set up in Calgary with the contacts I mentioned yesterday. They seem to be concerned and a little on edge due to the gang killings and increased police awareness. It seems as though there is another murder every day. But in some ways, that could work to our advantage. There could be some issues that we might have to deal with. I will know more about this in a couple of days. For now, that's all I can offer you. Are you going to miss me?"

Drake turned toward the fridge so the boss couldn't see his smile. He was glad the houseguest was leaving. He opened the door and felt the coolness escape as he grabbed a couple of beers. Before he turned his attention back to the boss, he dropped his smile and thought, *Not really.* Then he turned and answered aloud, "Oh, yeah, I will miss you terribly. Do you want a beer?"

"Now I know you are pulling my leg. Yes, a beer sounds good. Before you ask, I'm leaving early in the morning. The job I asked you to do has to be done ASAP."

"No problem with that. I have it all figured out. It will be done before you get back."

The boss stared at him, making him uncomfortable. Luckily, Drake's cell phone rang, and he was thankful for the distraction. He picked it up from the counter and checked the display. More news; *hopefully it will be good.*

"Hey, what's up, Ned?"

"The lady didn't like her gifts. There's a good indication that she won't be sticking around long. I'll get back to you when I'm sure."

Drake hung up and looked at the boss. "Mary didn't like her gifts. There should be some movement shortly."

The two men popped the caps of the beer and chugged half their bottles. "Let's just hope that Mary will head this way," the boss commented.

Drake smiled and said, "Where else would she go?"

"You're very confident. I hope you're right. As long as your sidekick doesn't get caught, everything should be fine. I have to make some calls, pack, and get things organized for my trip tomorrow. I'll catch you later."

"Yeah, I hope you have a good trip. I'll head out for a ride after I finish my beer."

The boss turned and left. Drake shook his head, *That man is always the doubter.* Drake would feel more at ease when that man left. He chugged the rest of his beer, grabbed his jacket, and headed for the door. He needed to cool off not only from the heat and the stuffiness but from being in the same room with the man who was full of hot air.

Now he had to come up with a plan to see that property. A ride would clear his head and help him think. *It's going to be an awesome ride. The job always seems to get in the way of my freedom. The things I do to make some cash.*

Chapter Sixteen

Mary trembled in the fresh air and felt she might be sick. *Calm, calm,* she said silently. The image of the faceless human form was imprinted in her memory. After a few more deep breaths with her eyes closed, her stomach finally settled. Slowly, she opened her eyes and glanced at the house she had left moments ago.

The sun glowed overhead. Its warmth indicated what kind of day it was going to be. The sun's rays felt great, but Mary was chilled to her core like a bottle of wine sitting in an ice bucket. She shivered as her thoughts returned to the blank face of the dummy lying on the carpet in her bedroom. The two officers were now outside and standing beside Mary. She felt the touch of a hand on her shoulder. Smith asked, "Mary? We can't imagine what you're going through. I apologize we had to put you through all that. Can you stay with Kath, or better yet, find somewhere else to go?"

Mary shuddered. "Yes. This is a nightmare. This isn't my home anymore." Mary looked away and shook her head. She stared across the street but didn't focus on anything. Her thoughts drifted from her house, the images, Jordie, and the person or persons who did this to her. The sadness of it all was discouraging. She needed a change.

She turned her attention back to the officers. They had been kind. "I don't know, can't think. Do we . . . do we have to stay here any longer?" She felt deflated, beaten.

"We'll take you back to Kath's house for now," Willcox said gently. "Do you have your keys? Smith will drive you, and I'll follow." Mary nodded. They assisted her up from where she was still kneeling. A shiver slithered down her spine as her body shook involuntarily; she was cold despite the sun. The officers guided her to her vehicle, and Smith opened the door for her.

Mary settled into the seat and put her head against the headrest. Smith and Willcox had their backs to her. She couldn't see what was being said and really had no interest. She closed her eyes for a moment.

The door opened, and Mary was aware of movement in the driver's seat. "Mary?" Smith asked, touching Mary's shoulder. Mary opened her eyes and turned toward Smith. "Where does your friend live?"

"The address is 220 Castlebrook Road, it's not far."

"I know where that is."

Mary turned her face toward the window. *What a beautiful day.* The sun was out along with a little breeze—a perfect picnic day. On days like today, she often thought of her sister. She missed Krisi terribly.

The vibration from the wheels was soothing. Mary felt relaxed and sleepy. When she shut her eyes, her mind drifted to the dummy in her house. But in her thoughts, the face was Krisi's. The lips were parted and it spoke, "Beware of danger." Startled, Mary suddenly moved. Smith stopped in front of Kath's driveway and looked closely at Mary. She quickly noticed that her pupils had dilated. "Are you okay?"

"Not really. I don't understand. Why did this happen? Who would do such a thing?" she asked and then looked out the side window.

Smith tapped Mary on the shoulder. Mary turned and faced Smith. "Mary, I have no answers for you. We're looking into what's going on. My partner and I want to talk to you further. Can we go inside?"

Mary nodded. They walked to the house. The parking stalls were vacant. She was still shaken. Her place could have been a scene from a horror show without the blood.

She opened the front door with the key that Kath had given her and stepped aside for the officers to enter. Mary walked past the living room and headed toward the kitchen. She turned to face her guests and noticed them staring at her.

"Did I miss something?"

"Why don't you have a seat? It looks like you are about to fall over."

Mary dropped into a chair and put her hands over her face. She wanted to get control of her emotions and not cry. Even though she felt helpless, she knew had to be strong. She removed her hands from her face and saw a glass of water placed in front of her. She reached for the glass and tipped it over. Water spilled everywhere, but most of it ended on her lap. As she jumped up, her chair tipped over and landed with a crash on the floor. Mary gasped from the bang behind her. The phone rang and Mary jumped again. She ran out of the room into Kath's bedroom and shut the door.

Willcox and Smith let the phone ring so the answering machine would take a message. Willcox glanced at the call display but the readout was name and number unknown. The beep of the machine kicked in, but no message was recorded. The only sound they heard was the hollow sound of a hang-up.

Mary returned to the kitchen in a change of clothes and was more composed. "I'm sorry. This situation has affected me a lot. I have to clean up this mess."

"Mary, please sit. There's no need to apologize. Smith has it almost done, and I think you ended up getting the worst of it. This isn't a pleasant situation. Let me get you another glass of water," Willcox said with a smile on his face.

"Before you do, I want to thank both of you for being with me today. It was nice to have someone with me. Also, I wanted to mention that there is a water bottle with a lid in the cupboard beside the kitchen sink."

The sergeant's laugh made Mary smile. "You look much better when you smile," he replied with a wink. Mary blushed and felt hot as the warmth spread from her neck to the top of her forehead. Feeling herself blush, she quickly turned her head. She had to look at something other than the man's eyes that she thought were so unique.

Smith sat beside Mary and patted her arm. "Now that's out of the way, we can continue where we left off." Willcox sat opposite Mary and gave her the bottle of water. She smiled in return and took a swig.

Smith looked at Mary, "I know things don't look so great at the moment, but they'll get better."

Willcox eyed Mary and added, "Is there anywhere else you can stay instead of here with Kath?"

Mary gave Willcox a shocked look. "Why? I'm comfortable here."

"Well, for one thing you saw what was left in your house, right? We don't want anyone else to be in danger. If you leave and stay elsewhere then that shouldn't be a problem."

"It sounds to me as though you suspect Kath. She definitely wouldn't do such a thing. She's like a sister to me and has been there for me so many times."

"We're not pointing fingers but keeping an open mind. We need to check out everyone you know, even your good friends. That means everyone."

Mary looked at the officers and shook her head, unable to believe what she'd just heard. She stood up from the chair. "Could you give me a minute, please? I'll be right back."

"Sure, Mary."

Mary turned and headed to the bathroom. She shut the door, leaned against it, slid her back against the wall until her butt touched the floor, and then wrapped her arms around herself. Even though the day was bright and warm, she was cold deep in her soul. *Who did this?*

Mary was tired and defeated from the morning's events. She needed to calm down. She stood up, walked to the sink, and splashed water on her face. When she dared to look in the mirror, it seemed that a stranger peered back at her. They have just come from seeing the mess in her house, but it felt much longer. She took a deep breath and slowly let it drain away. *I want this over with, the sooner the better,* she thought *Strange, just yesterday I thought a change of scenery would do me some good. Was someone reading my mind?* She didn't have to think twice about what to do now even though she felt like she was moving back in time, not knowing if it was such a good idea.

She kept going over the same questions that popped into her mind, *Who did this and why?*

Chapter Seventeen

As nightfall replaced the sun, Drake returned from his ride and parked his beast in front of the house on the small, square cement pad. Other than one dim, beckoning bulb that hung bare above the front door, the house was in darkness. Drake got off his bike, turned, and listened. The nights were so quiet. There wasn't much traffic on the road in the evenings. The silence was interrupted by howling coyotes in the farmer's field about a mile away, but the sounds seemed to be closer and were disrupted by a hooting owl.

He scanned the front yard and noticed the boss's truck was gone. He grinned and thought, *Right on, right on, maybe the man had to leave early.* Nothing in the yard seemed out of the ordinary. He couldn't have been happier or felt luckier at that moment. A drink was needed for a celebration without someone breathing down his neck. The weed last night was awesome, but he couldn't remember what happened after that. It was as though he had blacked out.

Drake entered the quiet house, switched on the light, shook off his jacket, and removed his boots. No one was here. He looked but saw no note, and no messages flashed on the machine. He walked into the boss's room and switched the light on. The first thing he noticed was that the man's laptop was gone, which was not surprising, as that piece of equipment was never left behind. He opened the closet and the breeze that it created rattled the empty hangers. The boss had packed up; it looked like he had moved on. Nothing was left in the bedroom to give any indication that the man was coming back. He smiled to himself and thought, *Damn, I should've bought a lotto ticket.*

As Drake left the room, the phone rang in the kitchen. He sauntered toward the ringing tone feeling sure he knew who was calling. He picked up the headset and said, "Hello" as he glanced at the call display but saw only a number that was etched in his memory. He was right, as usual.

"Hey man, what's shakin'?"

"I was about to ask you the same question. What happened to you? I thought you weren't leaving until the morning?"

"Something came up. The heat in Calgary is unbearable. The place is crawling with cops. My associates want to meet in Edmonton. I'm on my way there, as we are meeting early in the morning. Not sure when I'll be back. We have a few issues to sort out. I wanted to remind you of the job I need you to do and to get it done."

"You mentioned the farmhouse, no sweat. What else?"

"Find out what you can about Mary and anything else about Krisi. After you're done, contact me with the details. I hope that our guests will be headed this way soon. I want to know when they arrive."

"I'll get it done," Drake replied, wanting to end the conversation. He was glad the boss wasn't around. Drake let the man ramble on as he zoned out for a moment.

"Drake?" Pause. "Drake, are you there?"

"I'm here. I thought I heard something, but it was nothing. You know you can't be too careful. I will let you know when there is some news."

"There better be some activity soon. I need to know what Krisi was hiding from me and the only way I'm going to get it is from Mary. I got to run. Don't make me wait too long for any information that you might have, I'm not a patient man."

"Chill man, chat with you soon."

Drake placed the headset back in its cradle. *Now I can relax and put a plan together,* he thought. *Why does the man want to know so much about Mary? Very strange.*

As he opened the fridge and grabbed a beer, he wondered what was showing on the satellite. His stomach rumbled. *It's time to eat. A man can't think on an empty stomach.*

*   *   *

The boss man hung up, thinking, *I have to keep the peon on his toes.* He knew Drake liked it when he was not around. But he had no time to focus on that now, as he had other issues to deal with at the moment. One of his best recruits had barely avoided getting busted and almost got hit by a bullet from an ongoing feud. At least, he was smart enough to leave the city before the heat got turned up. This situation had to get back in control. All this activity couldn't have happened at a worse time. He knew this meeting had to go well.

Then he smiled when he thought about last night. Drake didn't know he was being used as a guinea pig. Mary Jane, who visited him, was a powerhouse. She was worth a mint. Plans had to be put in motion to have it flowing into the customer's hands. Tomorrow would be a good day if everything goes according to plan.

He was more than halfway to Edmonton, traveling on an endless ribbon of flat highway. The wheels hummed incessantly beneath him, and with nothing to see, he was bored out of his mind. The highway was almost deserted except for a few semis that he glided by. He switched on the radio. The station crackled as he passed through Red Deer, which was the dead air zone for the Calgary radio stations. He changed to another station to get some music. Ironically, the radio station was playing a favorite song that he used to hear when he was with Krisi. His thoughts returned to some of the happier times they had together. *Why had she left so suddenly? What was her secret?* He had to get some answers and was counting on Drake to provide him with that information.

Chapter Eighteen

Mary sat down and looked at one officer then the other. "I've decided that Jordie and I will be leaving Calgary in a few days. There's a lot to do and I need to make phone calls. Is there anything else you need from me before I get started?"

Smith replied, "We are glad to hear that there is a place for the two of you to go. Where are you headed?"

Mary had made the decision to move back to the farm where she grew up, thinking the change would be good for the two of them. "The farm where I grew up is in a small community about an hour from Calgary and is a quiet place."

"That sounds like a wonderful idea. Will you stay with Kath until you are ready to leave?"

"I would like to stay, but I need to talk to her about this first. I don't want to make another move before we leave." She wasn't as confident about the decision as she sounded. Some of the painful details of growing caused her to have second thoughts. She remembered the boys and girls teased her and called her fat. Her sister was always everyone's favorite. Krisi was the one who always got all the attention—especially from the boys.

Now that she was older, she looked much better, but it still hurt to remember those times. She was a bit nervous about putting herself back in that environment, but a lot of the kids she grew up with had died, moved on, or stayed put. She probably wouldn't see them that often. She was happy she had left, but everything would change now.

The house in Calgary had to be renovated because of all the damage. At the moment, she didn't want to be around it. From the looks of their belongings, there wasn't anything that could be salvaged. She wanted to leave as soon as possible, but there was so much to do in a very short time. She knew she had to take it a day at a time. Sighing, she took a deep breath and slowly released it as the tension seeped from her bones.

Mary felt a tap on her arm. "Mary, are you all right? It looked like you left us for a minute there."

"I'm sorry, I was just thinking of some unpleasant memories from the past. Now I should be focusing on the present."

"We'll send an officer around to keep an eye on you. Could you do us a favor?"

"What's that?"

"Be sure to keep the security alarm set while you're away or by yourself. If you notice anything out of the ordinary, contact us right away.

"I'll do that." Now that she decided what she needed to do, she wanted to be by herself to get her plans started.

"We need a list of your friends, ex-boyfriends, or anyone else that you can think of so we can check into them to see if anyone did this to you."

"Can I fax this to you if I don't get it done before you leave? I have a lot to think about it."

"Sure, Mary. We'll stay here until Kath gets back."

Mary thought, *Oh great, I have to play hostess. I'm not in the mood and really don't want to have company. I hope Kath will be back shortly.* "Can I get you anything, drinks or something to eat?"

"No thank you," they both replied. Smith asked, "Do you mind us hanging around?"

"No problem, but do you mind if I get started on my tasks? Do you want to watch TV? The remote is on the coffee table. I will be down the hall, first door to the left if you need anything. If you get thirsty, you know where the glasses are."

"That's okay, thanks," Smith said.

Mary went to the bedroom. She found some paper and a pen. Who could she put on the suspect list? She didn't think any of her friends would harm her, but then again, she didn't have a lot of friends. No relatives lived close by. She had met some relatives, but it was a long time ago and hard to remember them.

Mary wrote a few names down, but it was as though she hit a roadblock. In her mind, all she could see was a brick wall being built. She shook her head as the thought of the wall seemed very silly. It was hard to think and very frustrating.

Her mind raced back to the scene at her house, which was not more than ten minutes from where Kath lived. She pushed the memory aside, stood, and walked to the window to look out. The street was empty of pedestrian traffic or any trace of vehicles. A slight breeze came in through the open window, but the day was warm.

The sunlight bounced off the top of a small metallic shed in the neighbor's yard. The reflection appeared like a knife. She thought of the damaged pictures and the gaping holes in the walls that seemed like empty eye sockets staring at her. She closed her eyes in an effort to get rid of the images. Slowly, she reopened her eyes; the images were gone. She turned, chuckled to herself, walked back to the bed, and sat down. She picked up the list and reread what she had written. No other names came to mind. The ones that she had written didn't jump out at her as anyone who would want to cause her harm or vandalize her home. Mary tossed the list aside.

Next, she started to write, making notes as the information flowed freely from her brain like the fast current of a river from the pen to the paper. She couldn't forget Krisi's boxes in storage. She had procrastinated with the task of going through any of them when the police gave them to her after Krisi's case was closed. She would do it when they were settled at the farm.

No time like the present to get the phone calls started. The first call was to her insurance company. Mary briefly explained what had happened. The agent told her to come into the office the next day to deal with the paperwork. He also reminded her to bring the police report with her. That was one down.

Next, she called John and Betty Ericson, the couple that lived next door to the farm who kept an eye on things. They were a wonderful couple and so full of life. Both were in their late fifties, but they acted and appeared younger. She hadn't seen them in quite some time. They didn't ask many questions when she phoned, which was a bonus. She didn't want to pass along a lot of information over the phone. Mary trusted the Ericsons, but she also knew things slipped out when people talked. The community had its share of nosy neighbors. The next-door neighbors would make sure things were ready for her and Jordie when they arrived.

She also needed to talk to Eva, the realtor, to take the property off the market. It was up for sale but not advertised. She had not been in a hurry to sell the farm, and now she had a reason to keep the property—she would have no mortgage or rent payments. She called the real estate office, but left a message when no one answered the phone. She couldn't remember the cell phone number and would have to wait until the next day to phone during the office hours.

Mary left the safety of the bedroom with her list and walked toward the kitchen. She noticed the two officers were talking but couldn't hear what was being said. *Perfect timing,* she thought as Jordie and Kath walked through the front door returning from Susie's birthday party. The officers stood as Jordie and Kath entered the house and introductions were made. Jordie was awed by the uniforms and noticed the guns in their holsters.

"You must be Jordie?" Willcox kneeled in front of him.

"Yes, I am. Is that a real gun?"

"Yes, it is."

"Is it loaded?"

"Yes, it is. But the safety is on, so I won't accidently shoot myself or someone else. We don't want anyone to get hurt."

"Yes, that's what my momma told me about guns. I wish my friend was here to see this."

"Yes that's true." Wilcox gave Mary a smile and she nodded back.

Mary didn't want the officers around much longer, as they were a reminder of what had happened yesterday. She didn't want to be rude, but she'd had enough of their company. "Jordie, the officers have to go now, and I really do need to talk to you about something," Mary piped in and wished the officers would take the hint and leave.

Willcox gave her a puzzled expression but smiled and looked back at Jordie. "Yes, your mom's right. We are busy and know your mom needs to talk to you." Willcox shook Jordie's small, fine-boned hand that was enclosed in his own. "It was a pleasure to meet you and Kath. Take care of the two girls, okay?" He looked at Jordie with a serious look on his face.

Jordie looked at Willcox and said, "I'm too little; they have to take care of me. I will do that when I get older."

Willcox chuckled as he stood up. "Okay, Jordie, you do that." Willcox looked over Jordie's head and asked, "Mary, can I have a word with you in private outside?"

Mary's eyes widened in surprise and she quickly said, "Sure."

They stepped outside the front door and closed it. Willcox looked at her with a twinkle in his unforgettable eyes. She smiled and said, "Thanks again for everything. Here's a list of names you requested." She handed it to him, and he took her hand instead. She felt the smoothness of his strong hand as his warmth traveled up her arm. *Damn, his eyes were sexy.*

"Mary, I hope you don't think this is inappropriate, but I would really like to see you again. Would you mind if I visited you when you get settled in your new house?"

Mary blushed at his question. She didn't want to appear too eager. "Of course you can, if you like. Maybe the house will be in order in a couple of weeks. I hope that's all right."

Gently squeezing her hand, Willcox replied, "No problem. I have your cell phone number and will definitely send you a text message. My schedule is fairly hectic for the next couple of weeks too, but I'll have a few days off after that. I look forward to seeing you again."

Mary had regained her composure and smiled as she said, "No problem." He released her hand just as the front door opened and Smith came out.

Smith said, "Take care of yourself and Jordie."

"I will, thanks."

As the officers drove away, Mary turned and went back into the house, thinking over the conversation that had just taken place. She locked the door and set the stay alarm. Kath looked at Mary questioningly as if to say, "You're going to tell me about this later." Mary laughed to herself and grinned at Kath.

"How was the party?" Mary asked Jordie.

"The party was fun. There was a clown and his name was Mr. Yup. He was funny and had a big, red nose and a tiny, floppy, red hat. He had big feet and kept tripping over them when he walked." Jordie giggled as he showed his mother what it looked like; Mary chuckled along. "He made balloon animals and mine popped on the way home. We ate pizza, cupcakes, and there were prizes. I didn't win anything, but I still had fun. Are we going to do that on my birthday?"

"That's one idea. We'll come up with something when your birthday comes along." Mary's forehead creased as she stared off in deep thought.

"What's the matter, Momma?"

"Why don't we all sit down so we can talk?" The three of them settled on the couch. "The reason the police were here was because our house was broken into yesterday. All of our things were destroyed." Mary paused and turned to Kath before continuing. "Thank you for letting us stay here. Hopefully, we can stay here for another few days. We can discuss that after I finish telling you what happened. The inside of the house is a mess. Many things were broken or busted up. Do you understand, Jordie?"

"I think so. Does that mean all my toys are bad now? What about my clothes? Do they know who did this?"

"Your toys aren't bad. It is just that you won't be able to play with them anymore. Your clothes are ruined. I have contacted the insurance agency and will go there tomorrow. Later we can go shopping for new things. It's very sad about our things, but they are just things. Nothing happened to us, so that is a good thing. We weren't hurt."

Jordie turned away from Mary and looked at Kath. His face was sad on the verge of tears. "Auntie, can we stay with you?" Kath grabbed Jordie and gave him a big hug.

"Oh, sweetie, don't worry. You and your mom can stay here as long as you need to. Now don't be a glum chum. Things will get better. It's just going to take time. I bet your mom did some stuff while we were out. But I think she could use our help now that we're back. What do you think?"

Jordie turned back to his mother. "Momma, is that person going to hurt us?"

"Jordie, don't worry. We have protection from the police, which is why I locked the door and put the alarm on. We can set the alarm while we're in the house, so all of us will be better protected. The thing we have to remember is when someone comes to the door, make sure we know who it is before we answer it and make sure the alarm is shut off when we open the door because the alarm will activate and it is really noisy. Does that make you feel a little better?"

"A little."

"Okay, now for some good news. We get to go shopping for new clothes and toys for you. What do you think of that?"

"Yippee, really?"

"Yes, really. There is one other thing. We will be going on a bit of an adventure in a few days. Okay?"

Smiling and nodding his head excitedly, Jordie asked, "What kind of an adventure?" Mary described what was going to happen and what needed to be done.

"Why don't we go out now and get some shopping done? We can put some clothes and toys on layaway and pick up the rest tomorrow. We can get some games and play those tonight. Are we ready to go to the store?"

"Let's go," everyone yelled in unison.

*   *   *

Drake relaxed in his chair when a thought popped into his head. If he was going to make this move happen sooner rather than later, he needed to give it a little push. He picked up his cell and dialed the number. "Hey, Ned, I need you to do something for me in a couple of days."

"What?"

"You know the package the boss is waiting for? If there isn't any movement from the house, I need you to make something get hot, but also make it look like an accident."

"How else would it look? Is there anything else you need?"

"No, but if you hear anything else get back to me."

Drake heard, "Roger that," and the drone of a dial tone.

Drake thought of the real estate agent who hadn't returned his call about the property. When the phone jangled in his hand, he glanced at the display. *Great timing*, he thought and answered, "Hello."

"Drake?"

"Yes, it is."

"Are you available to look at the farmhouse at 8 a.m. tomorrow? I'm only available until 10 a.m. and have appointments after that for the rest of the day."

"That would work. Could we meet at the house?"

"Excellent idea, I will see you then. Have a great evening."

"You too, 'bye now." Drake pumped his arm in the air as he said, "All right." *That was easy. I need to find out some answers, and tomorrow is the day I'm going to do it.*

Pleased with the progress, he decided on another drink to celebrate. *Right on, right on!*

Chapter Nineteen

Mary woke suddenly from a deep sleep and jolted upwards. The dream had wakened her. She glanced at the clock on the nightstand. The red, glowing time of 4:00 a.m. stared back at her. Already, the dream had disappeared from her hazy memory.

She laid her head back on the pillow and closed her eyes. She took slow, deep-cleansing breaths to relax and clear her mind. The breathing exercise didn't work. She flipped on her right side and tried it again. Nothing happened. She turned to her left side. By now she was wide awake. The clock face stared back at her; thirty minutes passed since the last time she checked. The prospect of sleep was long gone. She decided it was time to get up and get ready for the day ahead.

Mary disliked getting up this early. She walked to the window and looked out between the slit in the drapes. She saw nothing but still blackness—just like her mood. She tried to remember the dream that awoke her. The somewhat familiar image of a man, more like a shadow, crept into her mind. Then the image was gone; the fragments were out of reach. The dream had left her with an uneasy feeling.

Mary turned from the window and decided to make the best of the early start of the day. She would use this time to exercise on the equipment in Kath's basement. It wasn't like going to the gym, but it still gave her the exercise she needed and would help clear her head.

Dressed in gym attire, she pulled her long, wavy, blonde-highlighted red hair into a ponytail and was ready for a workout. She knew she usually felt better after sweating away the stress that invaded her mind and body. She grabbed some water from the fridge, her running shoes, and trudged downstairs. She was having second thoughts about the move to the farm. *For now,* she thought, *this will be a short-term adventure.*

She switched on the TV and found a program she could watch with closed captioning while she did her exercises. First, a hundred sit-ups. Then she did her stretches. Before getting on the elliptical, she changed the channel even though she wasn't watching the screen. Rarely was anything of interest on TV at this time in the morning, as she had noted from her previous sleepless mornings. Her thoughts returned to what had happened to her life in the past few days.

Mary finished the elliptical and hopped on the stationary bike. She tried to focus on the program, but her mind reeled back to more thoughts of what was going on with Willcox and her house.

Kath had mentioned last night that her mom, whom she hadn't seen in a long time, was coming to visit and told Mary she was more than welcome to stay. Kath would purchase another bed or sofa bed for the basement. *Not on my account*, Mary thought. She had no intention of intruding on Kath's family time. Aside from that, other relatives would be coming and going all summer and Mary didn't feel comfortable with a lot of strangers around. Besides, Kath had enough on her plate with more people staying or visiting.

Mary needed to phone the insurance company to find out how long it would take to get things fixed and back to normal. At least the wall color could be changed. That was a bonus but what a way for it to happen.

Her exercises were finished and she headed for the shower. A list was needed to see what could be accomplished today. She definitely needed to make some phone calls and do more shopping. That was one activity that was bound to make her feel better.

Mary suddenly thought, *Be careful what you wish for. Sometimes those wishes come true—just like when I thought I needed a change of pace. Now it looks like it's going to happen.*

Chapter Twenty

Drake woke up before his annoying alarm clock came to life. He was fully awake but glanced at his bedside clock. It was 7:00 a.m., which gave him an hour to get ready for his appointment. He needed to make a good impression. Hopefully, she was hot. It wasn't so much the face that he looked at; he liked legs. When he saw a woman with long, slim, muscular legs, he knew she kept herself physical in more ways than one. He stopped daydreaming; it was time to move.

Once Drake showered and dressed, he was ready to roll. He just needed to find the key to the car that was parked in the garage. First, he searched the kitchen cabinets and slammed the last door closed when he came up empty. He opened the small drawers and looked inside but still no luck. Oh yeah, now he remembered where it was. He walked to the boss's bedroom and opened the top drawer of the small dresser by the bed and found the key. With one last look in the mirror, he was on his way.

He walked to the car, opened the door, and flopped into the seat. This plan had to go off without a hitch. He had asked a few of his friends to make calls to the agent while he was on the property to keep her busy and give him time to snoop around. He was looking for information but didn't know what it was or where it might be.

It was 7:30 a.m., and he would be there shortly. He had a feeling the real estate person would be early too.

By arriving at the property ahead of schedule, he could search without being followed around. Drake parked the car and scanned the buildings that were barren of paint and some that weren't quite erect. He had to move quickly, as he guessed he had about ten minutes to spare before the agent arrived. The lingering scent of freshly-mown grass hung in the air. He saw a large garden that was starting to grow. He recognized the sprouting corn, carrots, green beans, and potatoes. Seeing the fresh vegetables brought back memories of the past. Nothing tasted better than fresh vegetables direct from a garden.

He decided to look in the garage first. He opened the side door, switched on the light, and noted that there wasn't much of interest to look at. There were rusty tools, broken shovel handles, spare car parts, and a lot of junk that no one took time to clean up. No boxes in sight. He mentally crossed the garage off his list.

He exited the garage and turned right to check out the next building. The windows of the derelict building were broken or missing their glass panes. The jagged edges of one window reminded him of a German shepherd with its teeth bared and ready to snap. The building leaned to the right. Some of the boards barely hung on with a rusted nail or two. One strong wind and the building would be down for the count. The building must not have been painted for some time; the dry, gray wood had cracked in many places. The building reminded him of himself, alone, no one to take care of it. *Enough of the self-pity,* Drake thought. He looked in the window and saw more junk, old machinery, and tools from long past. Some of the stuff might be worth something to someone. It would have been interesting to see if there was anything of value, but he didn't have the time to check into it further. He glanced at his watch and figured he had about five more minutes before the realtor would arrive.

He walked a few steps away, toward a newer Quonset. The huge, sliding doors were open. He found the light switch and turned it on. He glanced at the combine, tractors, and a couple of big trucks. The floor was dirt. A few fine cracks in the foundation walls ran along the edges and looked like tendrils of vines growing upward. Not seeing any boxes, Drake backed out of the building. The air was clear, and he could hear the sound of an engine approaching. He glanced at his watch; she was early. He moved swiftly back to his car and waited for the vehicle to arrive.

A black Dodge Dakota pulled to a stop behind his car. The realtor was fairly decent to look at, her face anyway. She got out, shut the door, and walked toward him with her hand extended. "Drake? I'm Ava, pleased to meet you."

Drake nodded but didn't want to be too obvious by checking her out. Her face was on the slight side, and she had stylish light brown hair. Her eyes were dark brown, and her body was in decent shape. Ava looked good in her jeans and boots. Too bad there was a wedding ring on her finger. He had her pegged in her early thirties. She made his day a little brighter. He had to behave and get back to what he had to accomplish even though he wanted to do something different.

"Hello, Ava."

"Shall we have a look at the house and then move on to the outside buildings? Oh, something came up, and there is one thing I need to mention. The owner might change her mind about selling. I will let you know when I find out. Do you still want to go through the property?"

"Yes, I would. I wanted to see the property before heading out of town for the next couple of days. What's up with the owner?"

"She's thinking of moving here. Are you ready?"

Drake nodded his head and thought, *Interesting news; now if I only knew for sure.*

"Let's get started with the house," the realtor suggested. As they headed that way, Ava brought out the keys for the front door and opened it, allowing Drake to enter first. "The furniture that you are about to see is for sale if the property stays on the market. The house does need some TLC, but overall it is in fairly decent shape. There are three bedrooms upstairs and one bathroom with shower and bath on the main level. The basement is for storage, I think. There is a cold storage for fresh vegetables. I'm not sure what else is downstairs, but we will find out soon enough. We're headed into the kitchen/dining room combination in the shape of a large letter L. As you can see, it is open and bright." Ava's phone rang. "Sorry, Drake. I have to take this, business is booming. Please continue to look around. I'll catch up with you shortly."

Drake watched as Ava walked out the door, and then hurried to look in the living room. No boxes anywhere. The living room was a huge rectangle with carpet, furniture, and TV. A piano stood in the left corner. Quickly, he moved around the corner and found the bathroom but didn't bother checking out the room. He found what he was looking for. Steep, uncarpeted stairs led upward. Taking the steps two at a time, he quickly made it to the landing. One bedroom was on the right and two more were on the left. He turned to the right and stood in the master bedroom. The floor of the large square room was covered in linoleum with a flower pattern of brown, tan, and white. He opened the closet door and saw only empty hangers. Shutting the closet door, he continued his search of the two large dressers. One was placed at the end of the bed by the wall; the other was on the right side of the room. He quickly opened the drawers, checking the insides and underneath. All of the drawers were empty and nothing was attached to the undersides.

He turned and headed to the other two smaller bedrooms. He went into the bedroom on his right next. The room had the same linoleum flooring. He looked in the closet, but nothing was hidden. He checked out the dresser, with mirror attached, but found nothing in the drawers or underneath it. He glanced out the draped window and saw Ava still talking on the phone. *That's a good sign,* he thought. *Keep her talking; I have more searching to do.*

The last bedroom had the same flooring and wall coloring as the others. It also contained a dresser, a window with more drapes, and another closet. He sped through the drawers of the dresser but they were all empty. But underneath the last drawer, he found a yellow five-by-seven-inch envelope that felt as though something was inside it. He removed the envelope from its location and stuffed it in the back of his jeans, covering the treasure with his shirt.

"Drake?" A pause. "Drake, where are you?"

Drake had been concentrating on what he was doing and hadn't heard the front door open. When he suddenly heard his name, he yelled, "I'm upstairs. I'll be finished in a minute." He replaced the drawer and pushed it shut. He opened the closet, which was empty like the other two. Unaware he had been holding his breath, he suddenly exhaled. He needed to appear calm and not give himself away. The sounds of Ava's boots clicked on the bare wood as she climbed the stairs. He turned and looked out the window. "The view is amazing, you can see for miles," he said as Ava stepped into the room.

"Yes, it is an awesome view. Whenever I come here, I always take a few minutes to appreciate the beauty."

Her phone chirped. "Sorry, Drake, it has been a busy morning. Please continue to look around." Ava turned around and descended the stairs as she answered her cell with "Hello, this is Ava."

Drake didn't think there was anything else he could search for in the bedrooms and decided to follow Ava down the stairs. There was only one area he still needed to search and that was the basement. As Ava headed outside again, Drake headed for the basement door.

He opened the door and turned the light switch on. He carefully descended the gray, wooden stairs that creaked under his weight. He felt he was getting closer to more information than what he had already found. He wanted to see what was in the envelope, but he didn't have time. Halfway down the stairs and to the right, he saw shelves with canned peaches, pears, jam, and empty canning jars. Straight ahead, he saw the furnace, washer, dryer, and a huge freezer against the wall. He also saw another doorway opening, but no boxes were in sight. He walked toward the doorway and felt for a light switch. He had to see what was beyond the entrance. He found the switch and turned it on. A bulb flickered and came to life. He kept his fingers crossed that it wouldn't burn out. He didn't like dark places; he never knew if anything or anyone was lurking.

The cement floor showed evidence of tiny cracks that looked like vines grown on a trellis. There wasn't much in the room except old car parts, vehicle batteries, spiderwebs in the corners, a few boxes, and another door that was closed.

The room felt cooler than the previous one. The closed door must be the cold storage area that Ava had mentioned a few minutes ago. He walked toward the five boxes to see what was inside. The writing atop the first box indicated it contained linen; the second and third boxes were marked as dishes, pots, and pans—they certainly felt heavy enough. *MARY* was written on the next box. Finally the last box showed the name *KRISI*. There was no tape on the flaps, so it was easy to peek inside. He opened the flaps and quickly searched through the box. He found pictures of her parents, her sister, and a picture of the boss when he was much younger. The boss had curly hair at the time. Drake chuckled at the picture and boasted out loud, "I still look better." He pushed the two photos aside.

He knew he didn't have much time left, but he dug deeper to see what else he could find. He found a book that looked like a diary. He pulled it out and quickly scanned the dated pages. He put the book beside the pictures and continued to search. He came across a sealed, white envelope with Mary's name on it. He put that aside as well. He heard the outside door open and heard Ava call his name. "Damnit," he quietly cursed. "I'm down in the basement, coming back up now," he called. He carefully stuffed the items in the back of his jeans pocket before closing the box and placing Mary's box on top.

As he left the room, he turned once again and stared at the box he had just searched. He wished he had a few more minutes to investigate further. He knew he couldn't push his luck any longer. He hoped whatever he found would be enough. He shut off the light and quickly took the stairs two at a time to return to the main level.

"Drake, I must apologize for not spending enough time going through the house with you. However, I just found out the owner is coming back here to live within the next day or so."

"No problem, I can see that you're very busy. I'm glad you gave me the opportunity to view the property even though there was a chance the owner would decide against it. Well, if anything changes, please let me know. This place has possibilities. Not only that, it gave me an idea of what the houses might look like around here. Wow, look at the time, its 9:30. You mentioned a meeting at 10:00; it's about time I let you go." Still making small talk, they left through the front door and Ava relocked it.

After Drake started the engine, he rolled down the window and waved. He was on his way to check the hidden treasures he'd found.

Chapter Twenty-One

The next morning, Mary looked out the bedroom window. She could tell it was going to be a hot and humid day. The sun shone brightly with its rays making the pavement hazy from the mid-morning heat.

They had accomplished a lot the previous day. She bought new clothes, suitcases, toys, and even a bicycle that was on sale for half price. Jordie would have fun riding it at the farm.

Last night, she had had a good conversation with Kath. She not only felt better about the farm but actually looked forward to the change. This morning, Mary phoned Ava from the Re/Max real estate office in Drumheller to notify her that the sale of the property would be put on hold for now.

Kath had taken Jordie out for a bit, which gave Mary the time she needed to accomplish everything she needed to do. The first load of laundry was done and packed. The second load was in the dryer. She put the toys in boxes and left them by the front door for their journey. She also prepared snacks for the trip, as Jordie was always hungry. She had books and games ready for his amusement while they were traveling as well. *Thank goodness the drive will take only about an hour,* she thought.

She contacted the insurance company and gave them a phone number where she could be reached. At least she wouldn't have to buy new furniture as everything she needed was at the farmhouse. She phoned Betty to ask her to stock the house with groceries and see if the house needed to be cleaned before they arrived. Mary wanted to leave the next morning, which would give Betty enough time to finish the tasks she phoned about.

Mary glanced at her watch and noted she had time to do her errands. Later, she would meet up with Kath and Jordie for an early dinner to thank Kath for putting up with the two of them.

She stepped out of the house but paused at her SUV and scanned the area to see if there was an unknown presence. Even though she didn't have that uneasy feeling or sense of danger lurking, she wanted to be sure that nothing was going to harm her. Still unsettled about the break-in, she felt that after tomorrow she would be more relaxed—at least that is what she hoped for.

Mary picked up the boxes containing Krisi's personal items from the U-Haul storage location, filled her tank, and returned to Kath's house. When she entered the house, she saw a blinking light on the answering machine. The message was from Betty stating that all was ready for their arrival. *Excellent,* she thought.

After finishing the second load of laundry and the packing, she zipped the suitcase shut and left it by the door. The afternoon went by in a blur, which left her with just enough time to visit the post office to change her address before meeting up with Jordie and Kath at the restaurant.

With everything finally done, she could enjoy the evening without rushing around. The night was uneventful and went by without a hitch. It was great to have a quiet moment like this one. Mary was tired by the time they got back to the house. Once Jordie was in bed, she hit the sack and quickly slipped into a deep sleep.

The next morning, the sun was shining without a cloud in the sky. Mary awoke and glanced at the clock on the nightstand. She was surprised that it was 9:30 a.m. She had slept through the night—a first in a long time. This was an odd occurrence, as Jordie, who usually was an early bird, would rush into her room, jump on the bed, and wake her. She knew Kath had already left for an early meeting and would be gone most of the day. She wouldn't be around to say good-bye. Mary was relieved by this, as she didn't want Jordie to be upset when they left.

Mary stretched and arose from bed as it was past time to start her day. She grabbed her housecoat and put in her hearing aids, then left the bedroom to see what Jordie was up to. She found him still asleep on the couch in the living room. Instead of waking him up, she decided to take a shower.

Once she had showered and dressed, she went back to the living room where Jordie sat on the sofa watching cartoons. "Hey sport, how are you doing?"

Jordie looked up at Mary. She could tell he wasn't a happy camper. Mary walked to the sofa and sat beside him. "What's wrong?"

Jordie looked at her with sad, puppy dog eyes. "Do we have to leave? I really like it here."

"I know you do, but Kath is going to be very busy with her family when they come to visit her in a few weeks. She is going to have a house full of visitors, and I don't want to be in the way. Do you think it is fair that we are here when she has other people she needs to pay attention to?"

Jordie shook his head.

"It's been great that she has had a lot of time to spend with you, but it won't be like that much longer. Our house needs to be fixed up and that could take a few months. We talked about this last night. I thought you were happy about going to the farm?"

"I don't mind that we're moving, but do you think anything bad will happen to us there? Do you think we'll be safe there?"

Mary had wondered the same thing, but she didn't want Jordie to know that. It would only frighten him more. "So far nothing else has happened to us since we left our house, so I think it was a one-time thing." *Let's hope for the best,* she thought.

"I've known the next-door neighbors, John and Betty, for a long time. They were there when I was growing up and are very excited about meeting you. I always had fun when I was with them and learned many different things. There are lots of things to see in the area where I grew up. Did you know dinosaur bones were found there? There is a museum that we can go visit that I know you'll like. We can go hiking and exploring and swimming. A ferry can take us across a river in our SUV. They even have produced movies in some areas."

Jordie's eyes grew wide. "Really?"

At least she had his attention. "Do you think I would tell stories?"

"Guess not."

"John and Betty have big trucks, combines, and tractors. They have cows, chickens, pigs, and horses. Would you like to learn how to ride a horse?"

"I would like to ride a horse. Can I ride a horse every day?"

"Probably, the horses need exercise. You can ask John when you meet him. So what do you think about moving now?"

"Will the animals hurt me?"

"Oh, sweetie. The animals will hurt you if you are mean to them. But you're not going to be mean are you?"

Jordie eagerly shook his head no.

"That's good. Most of the animals are tame, but some of them are stubborn. You need to be careful and not get in their way. John will show you the right way to do things and tell you which animals are more difficult than others. What do you say we give it a chance and see what happens?"

"Okay, Momma, I'll try."

"That's my boy. Do you want to help finish packing up the SUV and then we'll go for breakfast? I'll let you decide where we should go."

"Okay."

Mary gave Jordie a hug and kissed him on the forehead. "Everything is going to be fine. Let the adventure begin."

Chapter Twenty-Two

Drake returned to his place with the items he had taken from Mary's house. At least, he learned that she was coming back. It wasn't clear when, but it had to be soon.

Placing the items on the table, he wanted to take a closer look at the pictures he now possessed. He still thought he looked much better than the boss did back then and, of course, now. Drake couldn't believe the boss's blond curly hair. It seemed like fine silk. No wonder the boss kept his head shaved.

Next, he opened the five-by-seven-inch envelope. It held a birth certificate dated August 10, 2005, with the name Jordan Charles Hill. He pushed the card aside and opened the envelope with Mary's name on it. Inside was piece of generic writing paper. He unfolded it and read the brief letter.

Dear Mary,

There were so many things I wanted to tell you the last time I saw you, unfortunately, my time got cut short, and I had to leave.

I was so grateful that you agreed to raise Jordie as your son. You were and still are the stable one. I couldn't believe that I got pregnant. I didn't tell you who the father was, but I'm sure you could figure it out. I didn't want him to know about the baby; he had changed so much just before I left. He'll always have a place in my heart, but I couldn't be with him any longer because of what he was getting involved in.

I did a lot of stupid things that I regret. The past can never be changed. I have to learn from it and move forward.

I'll remember the times when we were younger, and life was so much simpler and no pressure. We had some great times. We became teenagers, drifted apart, and I didn't treat you like a sister that I should have. You were always there for me and always had my back. I took all that for granted. I want to apologize for all the lousy things I did to you. I really miss you.

I hope you and Jordie are doing well. Please give him a kiss and a hug from me; tell him his other mom loves him. The both of you are in my thoughts and in my heart every day.

Take care of yourself, sis.

With love from the bad twin, Krisi

Drake put the letter aside and picked up the other pictures he had found. There was a picture of Mary and Krisi when they were about ten years old and had their arms over each other's shoulders. Without a doubt, Krisi was the pretty one. Mary was plain and not as striking as her sister. Drake wondered what Mary looked like now. He was sure it wouldn't be a mystery much longer. He picked up another picture and flipped it over. He saw Krisi with a younger version of the boss. It looked as though they were in their late teens—smiling, happy, and not a care in the world. He wondered what had torn them apart. *Oh, yeah, the man had changed.* What a shame.

He reached for the diary, curious as to what surprises this little blue book held. He decided to get comfortable, as it could take a while to read the diary. *It could be a fascinating read,* thought Drake as he reached for a beer in the fridge and made his way into the living room and his recliner. He twisted the cap off the brew and noisily gulped down about half of the bottle. He let out a belch and put the bottle down. He pushed the lever back to extend his legs in the upward position, opened the diary, and began to read.

Most of the writing involved Krisi's daily events. It was easy to read. It didn't take him long, as most of the entries were short, and some days she didn't write anything. Not much of what was written held his interest until the end. Krisi mentioned that she left the boss and hooked up with Rick. Of course, he was just a friend, yeah right, whatever. He flipped to the last page where she wrote that she could never let him know the truth.

Who was she writing about and what couldn't she tell? Drake wondered. *Just when the diary was getting juicy, there was no ending, damn it. There has to be another diary someplace.* He wished he could have had more time to search.

Something dawned on Drake; he turned the previous page and reread what was written. *Boss, you S.O.B.* Now he knew who was at the bottom of the coulee.

Drake's cell phone rang. He glanced at the display and answered, "Hey, Ned, what's up?"

"She's on the move and should be there in about an hour."

"Thanks for the heads-up." The conversation was over; the dial tone droned. Drake pressed the disconnect button thinking, *I'm going to take a ride shortly and check things out.*

Chapter Twenty-Three

Mary and Jordie were packed and had just enough room for the new items from a few days of shopping and the boxes she had picked up from the storage unit.

"Momma, can we go to McDonald's now?"

Mary looked at her watch and saw that it was 10:30. "Are you hungry?"

"Yes."

"Okay, sweetie, let's go."

Jordie quickly climbed into the front and put on his seat belt. Mary scanned the area to see if anyone was watching them, but nothing was any different than any other morning.

"What are you going to have for breakfast, Jordie?"

"I'm not sure yet."

Mary looked at Jordie and could tell he still wasn't convinced about leaving the city. She could only hope that once they had reached their destination he would have a change of heart. She took his chin between her finger and thumb and turned his face gently toward her. "Jordie, you know this is not a permanent move. We're going on a minivacation in an area other than the city. Kath is going to be busy with relatives and friends who will be visiting her over the summer. You know she won't have a lot of time to spend with you when that happens. I have a surprise for you. Since you're so glum, I'll let you know what is. But you have to promise that you will be surprised when it happens. Can you do that for me?"

Jordie looked at her and nodded.

"Kath promised that she would come to visit us in the next couple of weeks before her family arrives. When she comes to see us, we can go to the museum to see the dinosaurs. I know you like dinosaurs, don't you?"

"Yes, I do."

"Great. Does that make you feel a little better?"

"Yes it does, I guess."

"Now what's wrong?"

"What about my friends?"

"Let's see, most of your friends won't be in Calgary either. They are visiting their relatives who live out of town. Some will be going to Disneyland and other places for a vacation with their families. You wouldn't be able to spend much time with them for the next couple of weeks. Could you give the farm a chance just for a short while?"

"Okay, Momma, I will."

"I promise it won't be that bad. You might even make some new friends. I've already checked into a few things. And don't try to get it out of me. I'm not going to tell you what they are."

"Can we go now?"

"Of course, I'm hungry, what about you?"

On cue, Jordie's tummy rumbled in reply to Mary's question. They both laughed.

Mary drove to the closest McDonald's. They entered the restaurant, ordered, and sat at a table. Once they finished breakfast, Jordie played in the indoor gym for fifteen minutes before they began their drive. It didn't take long for Mary to leave the city, as they were close to the outskirts.

To pass the time, Mary told Jordie all the things that she and Krisi used to do when they were growing up. She described their pets and the horses they rode. She glanced at Jordie and noticed his eyes were closed. He seemed to be sleeping. She stopped talking and looked out the window at the scenery. Everything was luscious green, and the grass swayed in the gentle breeze. In the middle of the ditch, telephone poles were lined up like soldiers ready to do battle. Birds perched on the wires; clumps of trees with green leaves stood erect.

The road signs displayed tourist attractions and the distances in kilometers to the towns ahead. Houses and buildings were surrounded by trees. Patches of dead trunks appeared among the live ones.

The roadside ditches contained murky water. Idle farm equipment with a For Sale sign was parked by the side of the road. White puffy clouds with a tinge of gray speckled the blue sky. Mary passed many semis advertising their hauled loads. The pavement was uneven and scarred with fine cracks. The completed repairs made the pavement look like a patchwork quilt. Most of the highway had the solid white and dashed lines that made the left and right lane separation easy to see. The smell of yellow mustard in the farmer's field lingered for miles. A fine dust clung to her windows after a half-ton truck passed her.

From the previous rain, pools of water had accumulated in the man-made ruts. Shiny granaries stood by themselves as though they were outcasts. Many old buildings had fallen down. Others, in need of repairs, were still standing, but their roofs had caved in. Barbed wire fences enclosing the herds of cattle in the pasture were in need of new strands. Birds pecking at the carcass of a gopher that was spread on the pavement scattered as Mary's SUV drove by. A red-and-white truck waited for its driver to return from a day's work in the field. Smoke billowed and circled upward from a flaring gas well.

Mary hadn't driven this road for quite some time, but the road and surroundings were all so familiar. Some things were never forgotten. The drive wouldn't take much longer. Jordie was asleep and she didn't want to wake him, so they would see Buffalo Jump another day.

In the last stretch of the journey, just before turning the corner of the lane that led to the farm, she noticed a man sitting on his chopper and chatting on his cell phone. She thought he was someone she knew, but couldn't place him. He slipped out of view as she continued to their new home.

Chapter Twenty-Four

Drake caught a glimpse of the female driver in the vehicle that passed by. When he had looked at a picture earlier of the two sisters together he wouldn't have known any better, he'd say it was Krisi driving the blue SUV. Mary looked identical to her sister now. She no longer looked like the awkward young girl in the photos he had found but had grown into a beautiful swan. Now that he knew the package had arrived safe and sound, he could contact the boss. He wondered what the next plan of action would be.

Drake returned from his short ride from spying on Mary. Just as he was about to dial his cell phone, it pulsated in his hand. The annoying tune of the ringer let him know the boss was calling. He didn't want to answer but knew the man would hound him until he did.

"Hello, dawgggg," Drake answered with a drawl.

"What's shaking at your end?" The boss replied.

"I'm fine; how are you?"

"I'm good, but enough with the useless chitchat. Anything of interest happening?"

"Since you've asked so nicely, the package arrived about twenty minutes ago."

"Excellent news; that's what I've been waiting to hear. I'll be back tomorrow and you can let me know what you found from your treasure hunt."

The boss had just finished a meeting with his contacts and his day brightened at the news he had just heard. His thoughts drifted. The sun was warm. The leaves on the trees and the grass were a deep green. Many girls wore short-shorts and bra tops that revealed a lot of skin. Too bad he didn't have more time to sit in the park and take in some sightseeing. The women in Edmonton were fine but not as first-rate as those he saw in Calgary. *What's a man to do? Too much work and no play can make for a very dull day.*

Drake said, "I did find some interesting information and can't wait to see what your reaction will be. How are things at your end?"

"There's been a slight change in plans and a few delays, but things went well overall. We should be able to start in a few weeks."

"That's good, right?"

"Yes and no. I'll tell you more about it when I see you."

"Is there anything you want done before tomorrow?"

"Not sure yet but wait around until I get there."

"Yeah, all right," Drake replied tentatively.

"You sound so happy about that."

"Now why wouldn't I be? I always get money or other things when you come back from one of your trips."

"I think that's the only time you're glad that I show up."

"My mother told me to always tell the truth. But yes, that is one of the reasons I like when you are around. There are a few others as well."

Silence was followed by the sound of laughter. "The main reason I like you so much is your honesty. You always tell the truth, right?"

"Hey, what's that supposed to mean?" Drake asked.

"Nothing man, nothing."

Drake bit his tongue before he added anything more. *That man can be such an ass,* he thought. *One of these days, he'll get what's coming.*

"Well, if that's it, I'll see you tomorrow." Drake hung up before the boss could add anything further. It felt great to hang up on him. He needed to clear his head with some air and a longer ride to figure out what he wanted to do. He knew it was about time he moved on or took a break from his boss for a while. He had enough cash stashed and could get a legit job if he wanted. He was sick of the BS. But where would he go?

*   *   *

Mary stopped the SUV beside the porch of their new home. Jordie was still asleep. She was thinking of Blackie, the dog her family had had. He was a mixed breed, a mutt, a German shepherd mix. She couldn't remember exactly how old she had been; it was a long time ago. Blackie had floppy ears, not like a purebred German shepherd whose ears stood straight up in the air. The puppy was six weeks old when she and Krisi got him. She had spent most of her time with Blackie and trained him to do commands and tricks.

She chuckled to herself as a long-forgotten memory returned. Charles, aka Chuck or the boss, was Krisi's main squeeze when they were seventeen. One day, he rushed up to Mary as though he was going to attack her. Blackie was very protective of his mistress. The dog bit Chuck in the butt and hung on for a couple of minutes before releasing its vise-grip hold. Surprised by the dog's reaction, Chuck had stumbled forward, bumped his head on the top of the fence post, and fell down on his side. He was knocked out cold for at least five minutes. Mary had felt terrible at the time, but she laughed to herself about it now. At least Chuck got what he deserved and stayed away from her when Blackie was around.

She felt a tap on her arm and glanced over to see Jordie was wide awake from his nap. His eyes twinkled with excitement as he took in everything around him. "Hi, sleepy head, did you have a nice nap?" she asked with a smile.

"Is this where we're going to live for a while?" Mary nodded.

Chapter Twenty-Five

Drake traveled at a steady pace on his ride, which allowed him freedom to think. He still hadn't decided where he wanted to go, but he knew he had to leave tomorrow ASAP. He also wanted the money his boss owed him.

The light disappeared as gray clouds blocked the sun. The day was decent even though rain was in the forecast and the next day was supposed to be more of the same.

Before he left, he would destroy the cell phone's SIM card but ditch the phone. He didn't plan on coming back or contacting the boss man because he didn't want anything more to do with him.

Noticing quite a few of the neighbor's vehicles and a few cop cars parked in front of the access to the lookout point, Drake brought the bike to a stop. Strobe lights flashed blue and red. Why couldn't this have happened after he left? It wasn't a good sign. He knew what was going to be found and, of course, he knew the boss wouldn't like it.

He nodded to Max, his Friday night beer drinking buddy, who stood off to one side. Drake got off his bike and wandered over to him. "Hey, Max, how are things going?"

"Things are great. Friday's around the corner, are we still on for a drink?"

"I'll have to let you know. What's up?"

"A skeleton was found in a car down the embankment."

"Wow, that's weird. Things like that happen around here very often?"

"No, not at all."

Drake shook his head slowly. "Very strange, do they know who it is?"

"No, but rumor has it that it was the man who owned the Mustang. I can't remember his name. The last time I saw him was late last year. I thought he moved away. I'm not sure if it's him, but it looks like it's his car. He didn't seem the type to loan his vehicle to anyone."

"Did you know him?"

"I met him every payday; we would get together and play poker. I thought you met him?"

"No, I don't think so."

"Weren't you here last year?"

"I've only been here for a few months. I arrived in February. Don't you remember we met at Old Grouches in town? Shortly after that, we had a wicked snowstorm."

"Oh, that's right. We had nice weather up until then, and you rode your bike when you arrived."

Both men stood in silence as they thought back to the storm. The amount of snow in that storm was unbelievable. It was bitterly cold at thirty below for three days. The winds were strong, and snow drifted across the highway in the open areas. Driving was terrible. More than a few vehicles slid into the ditches and remained there for days. Power lines were downed; phones were out of service because the phone lines were laden with heavy snow. Ten-foot snow banks were common. People were snowed in their houses for about a week.

"Oh, yeah," Max said. "Now I remember. The weather was something else. It was like a freezer. I didn't go far except for those few trips to town. We haven't had weather like that for ages, and I hope it doesn't come back like that again. You must've brought it with you when you first came here." Max eyed Drake with a sly grin.

"Hey, that's not nice," Drake replied. "But I guess you could look at it that way."

"Drake, I'm pulling your leg. We always have a storm around that time of the year, but it's usually not that extreme."

"I'm glad to hear I wasn't responsible for that havoc. Hey, I got to run. I'm waiting for a phone call and didn't bring my cell with me. After you're done here, drop by for a brew. I can barbeque some steaks too."

"Well, that's an offer I can't refuse. I'll take you up on that, but I won't be able to stay long. I could be here another hour or so, though, to find out more about what happened."

"No problem. You can update me while we have dinner." He scribbled his phone number on a scrap of paper and handed it to Max. "Give me a call before you leave so I can start cooking."

"Yeah, no problem. Catch you later."

Drake nodded his head at Max and strode back to his bike. It was a good thing he was on his way elsewhere. He remembered that day in November. It should never have happened, but there was nothing he could do to change it now. He had to focus on the present and get through tonight. In the morning, he would get his money and get the hell out of Dodge. His plans had definitely changed now. The temperature in the area would get a lot hotter, and he didn't want to stick around. When the boss found out, he would be livid.

* * *

When Mary and Jordie stepped out of the SUV, she watched her son's reaction. He had never been on a farm, and many things were new to him. Jordie turned to Mary, and his mouth formed a perfect circle as he said, "Wow! Look at the tractor. It's just like the one in my coloring book!" He looked around and asked, "What's that over there?"

"Slow down, Jordie. You're talking away from me, you know I can't understand anything that you say, but what you're pointing at is a combine."

"Sorry, Momma, I forgot. What does a combine do?"

"It's okay. A combine cuts down the crops in the field when they are ready. It separates what's useful and what isn't. The good parts go through the cylinder on the side of the machine. The seeds are pushed through the long part and are emptied into a big truck. After the truck is filled, the driver takes its load and stores it in a granary."

"I want to see that happen."

"I'm sure you will. Let's explore. Ready?"

Jordie took off ahead of Mary and ran to the gate. The once cherry red barn was in view. The sun had faded the color; it was sorely in need of paint. Even the dark grey roof had faded. These tasks took money and time. But now that Mary was here, she would think about having it done. Maybe she could do some of it herself and John would know who she could hire to help with the painting. She still wasn't sure if she wanted to sell the property, but she knew making any kind of improvements would be better than the way it was now.

Walking by the barn, if Mary remembered correctly, there should be a sled that she and Krisi had used on many occasions in the winter. They'd had a blast sledding down the hills. The snowy winters had been wonderful. She remembered building a snow fort and having snowball fights. They could play in the fort for hours especially when it wasn't so cold. They pretended to be in a faraway mystical land where dragons and other dangerous prehistoric creatures roamed the earth. These memories brought back thoughts of her sister; she missed Krisi a lot. When Jordie looked at Mary a certain way she could see the resemblance.

Jordie stood at the fence and looked between the slats of the gate. He must have seen the cows eating the hay that was laid out for them to munch. Mary stood beside Jordie and looked at the building that was about fifty feet away. She remembered that Krisi and she had done the same thing when the building was brand new. Their dad had built it for the hogs. Mary remembered the variety of animals her family raised on the farm. Like other farmers, his family relied on the milk cows, beef steers, pigs, and chickens for most of their food.

Mary felt a tug on her shirt sleeve. Jordie was excited again. He pointed at the horses in the corral. Mary knew what he was thinking and said, "Those are John's horses. He will teach you how to ride starting tomorrow. You'll be able to ride when he is here. He wanted us to get settled first."

"Yippee, I get to ride a horse!" Excited, Jordie jumped up and down and added, "They look big." She didn't know where all his energy came from. He seemed to have an overabundance of it and wished some of it would rub off onto her.

She led him away from the horses and walked past a dugout filled with murky water. Mary showed Jordie that the ground close to the water's edge was very soft, which caused a lot of suction when a person walked in the mud. She explained that if his foot got caught in it and he tried to remove it from the gooey mixture, it could be an impossible task. The ground could rip the boot off his foot and keep it encased in the foundation of slime. Jordie's eyes grew wide. "Really?"

"That's right. You don't want to be stuck in the earth, do you?"

"No way."

After the quick tour of the farm, they returned to the SUV to carry their suitcases, boxes, and other items into the house. It was mid-afternoon and would take a couple of hours to get things unpacked. By the time they were finished, it would be dinner time.

Jordie looked at the truck that appeared on the lane. The truck was a royal blue 1951 Chevy half-ton. The rebuilt engine purred like a kitten. The ground was so dry that a cloud of dust trailed the vehicle as it approached them. "Who's that, Momma?"

Mary recognized the truck and the two people inside the vehicle. John had rebuilt the truck a few years ago and was proud of his restoration. "That's John and Betty—our next-door neighbors." She knew they wanted to welcome them.

Once the truck stopped, the couple got out. Mary gave John and Betty a hug and introduced Jordie. "Well, hello young man," John said.

"Hello," Jordie moved his head from John to Betty.

"What do you think of all this?"

Jordie looked all around and blurted out, "Sir, can I ride the horses?"

"You can call me Papa John. And yes, you may ride the horses when I'm here and that will be every day. I want to teach you how to mount a horse, control the reins, and walking around the horses. There are a few chores you need to do as well, feeding them, putting the bridles away, brushing them, and giving them treats. There could be other things as well."

Jordie looked up into John's eyes and said, "Papa John, I think I can do what you ask."

Mary chuckled to herself and looked at Betty who had an amused smile on her face.

"Okay, Jordie. You and I are going to walk and talk about the tasks that I want completed. I will give your mom a list after we're finished."

Once John and Jordie left, Mary and Betty had time to get caught up. Half an hour later, the man and little boy came through the door and entered the dining area. Jordie had a big smile on his face. John handed Mary the list and said, "I'm sure Jordie won't need anyone to remind him what needs to be done, but here's the list." Mary glanced at it and nothing seemed too hard.

Jordie tugged at Mary's sleeve and said, "Momma, guess what?"

"What?"

"Papa John showed me something, but I can't tell you what it is. You'll need to see what it is."

"All right." Mary glanced over to John and noticed a twinkle in his eye, and wondered, *Now what the heck is Papa John up to?*

Chapter Twenty-Six

Drake is such a dumbass, Charles thought. He couldn't believe that Drake would dispose of the garbage so close to the rental property. *What the hell was he thinking?* Charles knew the area would be buzzing with the news and crawling with cops for a while. When anything unusual happened in the community, everyone was interested and watched newcomers like hawks.

Charles wanted to spread some product in the area but that needed to be put on hold. It was time to move. Before he did, he needed to deal with the other matter, Krisi's sister, Mary. Perfect timing for the skeleton found, at least he wasn't in the area at the time when Drake did the job.

He mulled over the problem thinking, *It's time for Drake to take a vacation, maybe a permanent one at that. Yes, well that would look suspicious with another body found in the area. What can be done with Mr. Drake?*

As Charles continued to think and stared out the hotel's window, he felt the vibration of his cell in his back pocket. He scanned the display. *Well, speak of the devil. Drake must have known he was being cursed.* "Hey, Drake, what's up?"

"You know that task I did late last fall? It came back to haunt me."

"Yeah, I heard about it. To be honest, you need to take a vacation. Business is finished here. I will be back early tomorrow morning." Charles sighed loud enough over the phone for Drake to hear.

"Yes, that sounds like a plan."

"Be ready to move when I get there. I'll have your money ready and then you can leave."

"I look forward to grabbing my cash and getting out of here."
Drake responded as he reflected silently, *I'll miss the money, but I
won't miss you. In fact, I'll be glad to leave.*

"See you tomorrow."

"Ciao."

Charles hung up and immediately dialed another number.
"Ned, I have a job for you. Drake will be leaving shortly after I get
back tomorrow. I want you to follow him. Find out what he's up to
and let me know. See you at six a.m."

He pressed the end button and muttered, "Drake has become a
liability; it's time to get rid of him."

* * *

Drake had an uneasy feeling that the boss was up to something
because of how the man had sounded on the phone. He knew to
trust his instincts. Drake spoke out loud, "He's got some plan for
me tomorrow, and I don't intend to stick around to find out what it
is. I'm out of here." But first, he wanted to see if there was any cash
lying around.

Drake's cell phone rang again. As he looked at the number,
he remembered that Max was coming for something to eat. "Hey,
Max."

"Hey, Drake, I have to cancel. I have to hit the road early
tomorrow so no drinks for me tonight. I have to leave about 8:00
a.m."

"No problem, Max. Do you mind if I catch a ride to the city
with you?"

"Sure."

"Great. I'll be by in about an hour."

"Catch you later."

Drake searched the house, kitchen, bedrooms, closets, and the
living room but had no luck finding any money. *Where else would
that dick hide his stash?* He went out to the garage and rifled through
the cabinets, tool boxes, and other things that were stored in the
area—still no money. Maybe he was wasting his time, but he knew

there was money around the house somewhere; his boss was never empty-handed.

While Drake was in the garage, he searched inside the car that he had driven the day before. He also searched the trunk. He noticed the spare tire wasn't positioned quite right. He lifted the tire out along with the windshield washer fluid, a jack, and a window scraper. He lifted the board that covered the spare and wasn't at all surprised at what he found. There were guns, ammunition, and knives, but no cash. He briefly considered taking one of the guns but realized it wasn't a good idea. He was going to fly and wouldn't have anywhere to dispose of it before he embarked on the plane. Unfortunately, he found nothing else held his interest.

He thought for a minute to determine where he should search next. He went back into the house and reexamined the boss's bedroom more closely. The only thing that was odd was a small safe that he couldn't open nor find the key. There was one last area that he hadn't looked through yet, and that was the basement. Basements were not one of his favorite places.

He remembered the basement in the house he grew up in. Most of it was dark. One day, his brother locked him in the basement on purpose. Some mistake. He thought of the mouse that skittered across his bare feet. He could still envision the white mouse with its beady, red eyes and hear the sound of the chirping crickets. This was very scary for a four-year-old. He had cried until his mom came in from outside and heard his banging on the basement door to release him from his lower prison. Ever since that time, he stayed away from creepy basements.

Well, at least there was no one else around. He trudged his way to the basement. The space was big with a few pieces of unused furniture. He felt sure he was getting close to what he wanted. He searched the drawers of the desk and found nothing hidden. *Damn, damn, damn.* He pounded his fist on the desk. Suddenly, something hit the top of his foot. He jumped. "What the . . . ," Drake said aloud and heard his voice echo in the emptiness that surrounded him. Looking down, he saw a key that might open a small safe. He picked up the key and ran his thumb and index finger over the cool, smooth metal. He remembered the safe upstairs.

He quickly took the stairs two at a time, walked through the kitchen, and glanced at the clock above the window. It was about ten. It was time to move, he didn't want to stay in the house much longer. His stuff was ready to go. All he had to do was get on his ride and leave. But first, he wanted to see if the key would fit. If it did, he wanted to know what was inside the metal box. He pushed the key in the slot, but it didn't turn. *Damn.* He removed the key and inserted the key in the opposite position. This time, it worked. He smacked his palm on his forehead and said out loud, "Homer moment, duh." The sound of his voice was comforting.

He lifted the lid and found what he was looking for. This is where the boss kept his stash. There were many bundles of cash. It looked as if the boss had saved for a rainy day. Well, Drake's rainy day had arrived; he would take his fair share.

He fanned through the stacks of bundled hundreds, fifties, and twenties. There didn't seem to be anything different about the money. He wanted to make sure before he took the money and left. He pulled out his wallet and took out a twenty. He examined the front and back of the bill, comparing it to a twenty from the stash. Everything appeared to be the same.

Drake grabbed a bundle of hundreds, two bundles of fifties, and two bundles twenties. After a second thought, he took another three bundles of hundreds and a few more bundles of fifties and twenties. *These should do nicely as my bonus*, he rationalized.

He quickly walked to his room where he opened his duffle and shoved the bills underneath his clothes. When the cell phone vibrated at his side, he felt a chill run down his spine. He didn't want to answer but knew he would. "Hey."

"Hey, Drake. Do you still need a lift to Calgary in the morning?"

"Max, I'm glad you called. I was about to leave for your house. Yes, I'd like to take you up on the ride. You still headed that way?"

"That's why I called. I need to leave around six instead of eight like I planned."

"Not a problem at all. I'm on my way shortly."

"Okay, Drake, see you soon."

Clicking *end* on his phone, Drake spoke out loud, "The sooner the better."

Drake was pleased that Max phoned because he didn't want to take the phone with him. Drake forgot he had the attached cell. He removed the chip, dropped it on the floor and stomped on it a couple of times and pushed it away with his foot. He tossed the phone behind him and it clattered to the floor.

Drake suddenly remembered the items from Mary's house. He would leave the pictures. He decided to keep the birth certificate, as it might come in handy later on. He tore the letter and the last few pages of the diary into small pieces. The boss would have to figure things out for himself—if he was smart enough to do so.

Drake knew the perfect place for the items that he had kept aside. He returned to the closet where he had found the cash and dropped everything on top of the open safe. In return for what he had just done, he grabbed another bundle of hundreds.

Drake gathered his belongings, keys, and double-checked the contents in his duffle bag. After putting on his boots and jacket, he opened the front door, turned his head and said out loud, "Thanks for the bonus, boss, that was very thoughtful. I won't see you around, good riddance to bad rubbish."

Once Drake was outside, he looked up and noticed the night sky was nothing but blackness. No stars were visible. The predicted rain was on its way. He could smell the scent in the air as he got on his ride, revved the engine, and gave the house a one-finger salute and thought *That's for you, boss man.*

Chapter Twenty-Seven

Mary was in the kitchen making pancakes. Jordie was still asleep. He'd been a busy little guy yesterday; she was sure he would be hungry when he woke up.

It was great to visit with John and Betty and get caught up. Mary had her fill of gossip about the neighbors even though she knew Betty liked to exaggerate. She would have to be careful of what information she passed along, as she didn't want everyone to know her business.

Without the help of John and Betty, it would have taken a lot longer to get organized. After they were done, they had a barbeque. She had forgotten that everything tasted so much better in the country air.

As Mary finished cooking the pancakes, she saw movement out of the corner of her eye.

"Hi, Momma."

"Hey, sleepyhead. I woke up before you this morning."

"Yes, you did. You're making my favorite. I could smell them cooking upstairs."

"That's right, I'm making pancakes."

"I'm going to ride a horse today."

"That you are. Looks like a beautiful day for it. The sun is shining, there's no wind, and the clear sky is a light blue. After your chores and your riding lesson, we can go exploring."

"Where are we going?"

"Now that's a surprise, but be ready to do some hiking. Are you ready for breakfast?"

"Yes. I'm hungry."

They had just finished when they saw Papa John drive toward the house. Betty wasn't with him today, as she was busy babysitting their grandkids.

Jordie ran out the door and yelled, "Papa John, how are you?"

"Hey kid, I'm good. Are you ready to go riding?"

Jordie quickly nodded his head. He jumped up and down and yelled "Yippee!"

"Let me talk to your mom for a minute then we'll be on our way."

"Okay."

Mary walked out of the house to greet John just after he and Jordie had finished talking. "Hey, John, how are you today?"

"Hi Mary, I'm fine. Would you mind if Jordie came over after we're done here?"

"Jordie, do you want to go play with Papa John's grandkids after you're finished?"

"What about our hike?"

"We can do that tomorrow."

"Okay."

John looked at Jordie. "Ready sport?"

"Yes." Jordie started to run toward the barn and suddenly stopped. He turned and ran back to Mary. She squatted and Jordie gave her a hug. "I love you, Momma. Are you going to miss me? Do you want me to stay with you?"

"I love you too. Sure I'll miss you, but I want you to meet some new friends."

"Okay, Momma, I'll go. I didn't want you to be lonely."

Mary kissed his forehead and said, "You're very sweet and thank you for thinking of me. I seem to remember I have some things that I need to get done. It would be a good time to do them while you're away for a little while."

Jordie took one last look at Mary before turning and heading to the barn again at a slower pace.

"Thanks, Mary. I'll let you know when we're leaving."

"Okay, thanks."

Mary watched the man and little boy make their way to the barn. She went back into the house and chuckled as she thought, *A couple of days ago, Jordie wasn't happy about leaving Calgary. Now he seems content about being here. I'll have to keep him busy so he won't be bored or miss his friends from the city.*

*   *   *

Charles arrived at the house and noticed Drake's chopper was gone. Maybe the shithead went for a ride and would be back soon, so much for telling him not to go anywhere.

When he noticed the garage door was open, he walked into the building and looked around. The garage had been ransacked. Cabinet doors were wide open, the contents lay on the cement floor. Tools were scattered everywhere.

What the hell is the trunk of the car doing open? He looked inside and saw his roadside accessories.

What the hell happened here? He rushed into the house and checked Drake's room. The dresser drawers were opened and emptied. The closet door was open; he stared at the naked hangers.

He turned, quickly walked to his room, and rushed to his closet. His safe was wide open. *I'm going to kill that prick.* Charles knelt down and determined what Drake had taken. Papers were torn in tiny pieces. He glanced at a couple of pictures. One photo was of Mary and Krisi when they were about ten. The other one was of Krisi and him. Her smile would brighten a dark day. He flipped through the diary and noticed the torn pieces were that of the missing pages. He'd have a better look shortly. He started counting the bundles of money; it was fifty thousand short.

Charles pounded his fists against the walls and quietly spat out, "That shifty little weasel, I'll get even with him eventually." He moved all the information that he had pushed aside on top of the money. He slammed the door of the safe shut and relocked it. He removed the key and stuffed it in the front pocket of his jeans.

He yanked his cell phone from the holder attached to his belt. He dialed the number he knew so well. He wasn't surprised that it rang continuously. That prick is either ignoring me or didn't take his phone. He hung up and quickly dialed another number. "Hey, Ned, what time did you park your ass outside the house?"

He listened intently. "Well, he's not here. Did you walk around the property when you arrived?"

The boss was speechless as he listened to the other side of the conversation. Words finally escaped his mouth, "Shit. It looks like he took off. I need to know for sure. Drive to his buddy Max's house and see if his rig is there. Get back to me when you have something to tell me."

He punched the *end* button and threw the phone on the sofa. *Think. Drake wasn't as dumb as I thought he was. I have to give him some credit for what he did.*

The ring tone came alive on his phone. He snatched the phone up and answered, "Hey."

The boss listened carefully and his facial expression turned into a scowl. "Thanks, you're the bearer of good news. I'll get back to you. Take off, but don't go far."

Charles thought about the situation. *Max's rig is gone, Drake parked his ride at his buddy's house, and they are not there. There's no one else that he hangs with in the area.* Then Charles spoke out loud, "Since there isn't anything more I can do about this situation at the moment, I'll need to make plans to get ready to leave and catch up with Mary. I know she'll be glad to see me."

Chapter Twenty-Eight

John and Jordie had just left and Mary was alone in the house. She felt a little on edge because no one else was around. She sensed something was about to happen—something she couldn't do anything to stop.

She had to think about something else. Baking would do the trick. Chocolate chip cookies sounded good and were Jordie's favorite. She thought about doubling the recipe if she had enough of everything and freezing the dough. When it was cooler, she would bake them. It was so hot today. Maybe it would be cooler tonight or in the morning. There were quite a few fans blowing recycled air, but they wouldn't cool the house enough when the oven was on.

She gathered the ingredients. As she measured them into a bowl, her BlackBerry vibrated in the pocket of her shorts. The display showed Kath had sent her a message wanting to know if she could visit on the upcoming weekend. *It would be nice to see her—what a great idea,* Mary thought. She quickly sent a return message asking what time she would leave Calgary on Friday and if she needed directions.

As she continued mixing the cookie batter, she remembered the time when Krisi and she were about three. The two girls were in the kitchen with their mom, who was doing the same thing that Mary was doing now. The current white, gas stove, however, was much different than the previous one. The old oven had a pilot light that had to be lit with a match. The oven got extremely hot and didn't cool off very fast. Her mother had gone into the living room for a couple of minutes after she had finished baking the cookies. Krisi followed their mother, but she did not.

Instead, she looked up at the top of the stove and saw something that caught her attention but was out of her reach. She stretched her tiny little legs as far as she could by standing on her tiptoes but still couldn't grasp it. Her hand slipped and her palm brushed up against the front door of the oven. It was very hot, and she remembered pulling her hand away quickly. A slight yelping sound escaped her lips. Feeling a slight burning sensation, she looked at the inside of her hand and was startled to see a big bubble covering the palm. The burning feeling had subsided, but she still felt the tingling.

She had stood quietly as she poked her finger at the bubble that felt soft and squishy. When her mother returned to the kitchen, she noticed her daughter's hand and screamed as Mary began to cry. Mary's mother took her to the clinic. After the examination was over, Dr. Bob put salve on her hand and bandaged it. He also gave her a red sucker that tasted like strawberries.

Her thoughts returned to the present. She glanced at her palm, which held no scars of the past. It was almost as though it never happened. At least, the oven was different now, and she was older and wiser when it came to using the appliance.

She looked out the bay window in the dining room and saw a deep red Honda Ridgeline driving in the yard.

Who could that be? she wondered.

Chapter Twenty-Nine

Charles was almost there. The day was clear and hot with no clouds in sight. Due to the lack of rain, the road was dry. The truck kicked up a cloud of dust as he drove on the unpaved road. *What was Mary thinking? I'm sure she'll be surprised to see me.* Today, he was going to find out what Krisi had hidden from him.

He stopped the truck next to the cement pad that led to the front door of the house. When she walked through the doorway, he was taken aback. *My god, she's beautiful and is the spitting image of her sister.* He almost dropped the cigarette that dangled from his mouth but caught it just in time. The hot end burned the tip of his finger. He swore under his breath. Mary had a smile on her face. Her smile reminded him of Krisi. Drake was right. If the two women stood side by side right now, he wouldn't have been able to tell them apart.

Mary sat down on the top step and waited for him. He opened the door and stepped out of his truck. He moved closer to her. He raised one leg and rested it on the second step. He bent forward so his eyes were level with hers.

"Hi, Mary, how've you been?"

Her eyes focused on his mouth as she responded, "I'm fine. Charles, what do you want?"

"That's no way to greet an old friend."

"You're old but not much of a friend."

Charles smiled slightly with a flutter in his gut and felt a little uneasy. He couldn't let her get to him. "You're very rude. Will you please get me a drink? It's a hot day, and I'm thirsty."

"Where are my manners? I wasn't expecting company—especially not you. The only thing I have is water. I just moved in and haven't had time to get groceries yet." It was a lie, but she didn't want to tell him otherwise. "I will get the water, wait here." Not waiting for a reply, she stood up and walked into the house.

As she filled two glasses with water from the fridge, she had to admit that while Charlie had been good-looking, he looked even better now that he was older. She remembered his piercing blue eyes. He looked as though he still worked out. His body was well sculpted, and his bald head made him even sexier.

She returned outside and handed him a glass. "Here is your water. Now what do you want?" She remained standing, waiting for his response.

"Isn't this much better, two friends talking?"

"Charles, let me clear something up for you. We were never friends and never will be. I knew you because you were my sister's boyfriend. As for being any kind of friend, you always made fun of me and were only around when Krisi was available. Now, I'm asking you again, why did you come? Spit it out and be on your way."

"You remind me so much of Krisi. You're an exact replica of her. You must know I still miss her."

"You've got some nerve. You're part of the reason why she's not here anymore."

"What?" Charles stuttered. "Me?"

"Yes, you. The reason she left was because of you. She knew you were involved in something illegal and didn't want any part of it."

"Okay, tell me something. I know the two of you weren't in touch much after she took off. So how can you be sure?"

"I have my ways. What's it to you?"

"I don't like to be blamed for something that wasn't my fault."

"You're so full of it!"

Frustrated, Charles shook his head and pounded his fist on the railing of the deck. Mary jumped. "Damn it, Mary, I truly cared about Krisi."

"That's what you say but actions speak louder than words. Now would you please tell me why you're here? Skip the BS and tell me the truth."

Mary stared at Charles and felt her resolve slipping. Whatever he wanted, she wished he would just say it. Charles returned her stare and realized he liked the new, feisty Mary.

"All right, your sister was keeping something from me. I don't know what it was."

"I wouldn't know anything about that."

"Did she send you any letters? The last time I saw Krisi was almost five years ago. She left me with only a good-bye letter."

"Why is this so important to you?"

Charles looked at Mary for a moment. He didn't know how to answer her question. "She left me a letter and probably left one for you as well. I just want to know why she took off the way she did."

"Yes, I did get a letter. But at the moment, I'm not sure where it is or even if I still have it."

"I'm sure you do."

"Okay, Charlie, what's going on? Stop playing games."

"I'm impressed with you. You've grown up and not shy anymore."

"I could care less about what you think of me," Mary replied tersely and looked away. She wanted him to leave, but he didn't take the hint. She felt a tap on her shoulder. At least, he had the sense to get her attention.

She looked at his eyes and realized that Jordie's eyes were very much the same. This can't be happening. She thought back to the conversations she'd had with Krisi. Not once had Krisi ever mentioned who Jordie's father was.

"Mary, come on. I don't want to be difficult, but Krisi was keeping something from me. Do you have any idea of what that might be?"

Mary sat down on the top step and began to shake her head. In her heart, she knew the secret. *Should she say anything?* Mary looked at Charles again and noted his expression was that of a lost little boy. She had seen the same expression on Jordie's face when he was troubled. She didn't want to feel sorry for this man, but she did.

He was persistent. She knew if she didn't say anything to him that he would keep hounding her. She hoped she wouldn't regret the decision she was about to make. "Charles, I think I know what Krisi was keeping from you, but I'm not 100 percent sure."

"Okay, what?"

"You will need to see for yourself."

"How long is this going to take?"

"Not long, I have to send a message."

"Can't you tell me?"

"No, I can't."

"You don't like me much, do you?"

"It's not a point of liking, it's a point of someone being trouble and that someone is you."

"Trouble's my middle name," he chuckled.

Mary rolled her eyes. "Yes, that's true. Wait here, I need to get my BlackBerry. I hope I'm not going to regret this." She went inside and sent a message from her BlackBerry asking John to bring Jordie home.

Charlie and Mary made small talk as they waited for Jordie to arrive. Within a half-hour, John's truck made it up the driveway. He stopped the truck and looked at Mary and then Charles. He knew something was up.

Mary opened the passenger side of the truck and said, "Hey, Jordie, give Papa John a hug and say good-bye."

"Okay. Bye, Papa John. I'll see you tomorrow!"

"Bye, Jordie, 'later gator." Jordie giggled as John put his truck in reverse and waved.

"Momma, why did I have to come back?"

"Well, Jordie, I'm sorry about that. I needed you to come home so you could meet a friend."

"Are we going back to Papa and Nana's?"

"Maybe later."

"Jordie, this is . . ." Before Mary could continue, Charles interrupted. "Hi. Jordie, my name is Charles, but you can call me Charlie. I'm a friend of your mom's."

"Which one?"

Charles looked at Mary with an odd expression on his face. He raised an eyebrow as if to ask, "What?"

Mary smiled. "Charles, Jordie has two moms. He knows that Krisi was his real mom and that she's in heaven. I'm his adopted mom."

"Well, that makes sense." Charles looked at Jordie's features; his eyes were almost identical to Mary's. His hair was curly and strawberry-blond like Krisi's. It was startling how much Jordie's overall appearance resembled his when he was a boy. He quickly realized this was the secret that Krisi had kept from him all this time. *Truly unbelievable; I have a son.*

"Charlie? What are you thinking?"

"I . . . I'm not sure what to think. Can we spend some time together before I leave?"

Mary thought about it for a moment and said, "Why don't we go in the house, where it is cool? Jordie, do you want a snack?"

"Yes, please."

"Let's go inside and get you one."

As they entered the house, Charlie kept thinking, *I have a son; he's a mini me.*